W9-BRK-174

DARIUS & TWIG

DARIUS & TWIG

WALTER DEAN MYERS

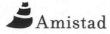

Amistad

An Imprint of HarperCollins*Publishers*

Amistad is an imprint of HarperCollins Publishers.

Darius & Twig
Copyright © 2013 by Walter Dean Myers
All rights reserved. Printed in the United States of America.
www.epicreads.com

Library of Congress Cataloging-in-Publication Data
Myers, Walter Dean, 1937–
   Darius & Twig / Walter Dean Myers. — First edition.
      pages cm
   Summary: "Two best friends, a writer and a runner, deal with bullies,
family issues, social pressures, and their quest for success coming out
of Harlem"— Provided by publisher.
   ISBN 978-0-06-172823-5 (hardcover bdgs)
   ISBN 978-0-06-172824-2 (lb bdgs)
   [1. Best friends—Fiction. 2. Friendship—Fiction. 3. Authorship—
Fiction. 4. Running—Fiction. 5. African Americans—Fiction.
6. Dominican Americans—Fiction. 7. Harlem (New York, N.Y.)—Fiction.
8. New York (N.Y.)—Fiction.] I. Title. II. Title: Darius and Twig.
PZ7.M992Dap 2013   2012050678
[Fic]—dc23   CIP
                                                                  AC

Typography by Jennifer Heuer
13 14 15 16 17 LP/RRDH 10 9 8 7 6 5 4 3 2 1

First Edition

chapter one

High above the city, above the black tar rooftops, the dark brick chimneys spewing angry wisps of burnt fuel, there is a black speck making circles against the gray patchwork of Harlem sky. From the park below it looks like a small bird. No, it doesn't look like a small bird, but what else could it be?

At the end of a bench, a young man holds up a running shoe.

"It doesn't weigh anything."

"That's the thing," Twig said. "There's going to be nothing keeping me back except gravity. When I hit the track in these babies, I'm going to be flying!"

"The heel is flat. Why doesn't it have a heel?" I asked.

"Because this shoe doesn't want my heels touching the ground," Twig said, smiling. "This shoe doesn't play. This is eighty-five dollars' worth of kick-ass running, my man."

"You paid eighty-five dollars for these shoes?"

"Coach Day got them for me because I'm on the team."

"Looks good, I guess," I said, handing the track shoe back to Twig.

"Hey, Darius, my grandmother said you should come by this weekend," Twig said. "I told her that you were really Dominican but didn't want to admit it."

"Why did you tell her that?" I asked. "I'm not Dominican."

"Right, but she thinks she's a detective," Twig said. "When you come over, she's going to break out into some Spanish in her Dominican accent and see how you answer. She thinks you're going to come back in Spanish, and then she's got you!"

"Why do you do stuff like that?"

"Because it's fun," Twig said.

"It's stupid," I said.

"A little," Twig said, smiling. "But it's fun, too. You saw Mr. Ramey today? You said you were going to talk to him about a scholarship."

"I saw him," I said.

"Didn't go too good?" The corners of Twig's mouth tightened.

"I ran into the numbers," I said. "He asked me what my grade-point average was, as if he didn't already have it. I told him it was about three point two, and he just shrugged and said it was closer to three even."

"You show him the letter from Miss Carroll?"

"Yeah, she already spoke to him about me," I said. "The thing I couldn't get around was that she was saying I'm smart—"

"You are, man!"

"Okay, but what he's saying is that when you send a transcript to a college, they want to see the numbers written down that say you're smart. Two point five isn't going to make anybody jump up and down unless you're six nine or can run a ten-second hundred yards wearing football cleats."

"Man, you got too much on the ball not to get a scholarship to some school," Twig said. "You tell him about the letter you got from that magazine?"

"How if I revise my story they might publish it?"

"Yeah."

"I showed it to him so he could see it was real,"

I said. "He got right to the bottom line. He said that right now I wasn't scholarship material. If the *Delta Review* actually published the story, I should come back to him and he'd call a few colleges. I don't think he thought I had a chance. The *Delta Review* is a college quarterly, Twig. It's got a lot of prestige, and everybody who's a serious writer is shooting for it."

"He's a cold dude, Darius," Twig said.

"No, man, it's a cold-ass world. When you open the refrigerator and you get cold coming out, you should expect it."

"That's all he had to say?"

"No, he said that maybe I should drop out and do my junior year over again. He said he wasn't recommending it but that I should maybe think about it."

"You going to do that?"

"No. I could run into the same thing I ran into this year and then just not finish high school," I said. "This way at least I'm on the track to graduating."

"You tell him why your grades were messed up?"

"I started to get at it, but he didn't want to hear it," I said. "He wasn't bitchy about it or anything like that, but he laid it out straight. He said that what I needed, a full scholarship in a school away from Harlem, just wasn't going to happen."

"So what you going to do?"

"Hope I can fix up the story so that they'll publish it," I said.

"You can do it, bro," Twig said. "I know you can do it!"

"He called up Miss Carroll when I was sitting there," I said. "He asked her point friggin' blank if I had a chance to get published. She said I had a chance, but the way she said it—"

"He had her on speakerphone?"

"Yes. The way she said it was like . . . she didn't much believe in it," I said. "She told him that they probably had hundreds of submissions and mine had to be one of the better ones if they were even considering it. She was pushing for me, but she was being realistic."

"What did Ramey have to say about that?"

"He said that the colleges wanted to know what *happened*, not what *could* have happened."

I watched as Twig laced on his new running shoes and tried them out on the track. He looked happy as he ran. I was watching him, but in my head I was replaying the conversation between me and Mr. Ramey, the school's guidance counselor. He had said a lot of things about how well I had tested when I entered the school, and how much promise I had. Then he went on about my chances for a scholarship. That was the short part of the conversation. I had figured it would be.

The thing was that I needed a scholarship that would get me out of my house, away from my mom, away from the hood, and most of all, away from the crap that was going on in my head every day. Mr. Ramey was right. It didn't do any good being smart. If you were smart and if the world had been right side up, then you would be rewarded for being smart. But the way the world really worked, the way it went down especially when it came to dudes like me, was that you had to walk a path to show you were smart, and it didn't have anything to do with what you had in your head or in your heart. It had to do with what you scored on tests, the grades you got, and what grades they could send to a college.

It was a struggle for me to stay in high school. My dad was living somewhere on the Lower East Side, drugging himself to death, and Mom was struggling with a string of cheap jobs that never paid enough to get by on. She was depressed and about a heartbeat from giving up. I had seen her like that previously. Before my father stepped—back when he was really reaching out to her—she had withdrawn inside and hidden away from the world. My father couldn't take it and moved out one Friday evening. Mom had cried herself to sleep for the next few days and then went even deeper into her shell. She had even talked about killing herself.

Up until then, I had done well in school. When crap came my way, I just pushed back and got by it somehow. It got harder. I had to look out for my brother, and for Mom as well. Then I just wanted to be away from the whole set.

At first I began to think of myself as a bird, flying high over the rooftops, or even a plane just passing from LaGuardia Airport on its way to Europe or Africa. But then, as the anger rose in me, I started thinking of things I would like to do to people who messed life up, who could take an ordinary day and turn it into something nasty and screwed up. That was when I began to think of birds of prey.

Twig didn't know it, but he kept me sane. In my

darkest moments, when I was feeling really, really shitty, I could think about him and his running and feel better about life. It was always good to see him smiling and trying to win his races. He had talent, so winning was possible. And if winning was possible for him, I felt I might cap a break, too.

chapter two

There is a slithering in the grass. The movements of the shadowed patterns are almost invisible in the small patch of bush, except from where I hover far above the earth. On the other side of the patch, a small brown animal moves away from the green carpet and along the winding edge of a stream. It is a paca. The paca stops near the base of a tree and lifts its head to sniff the heavy, humid air. Suddenly it stops, frozen in the moment, listening to whatever is moving through the dewy grass. The paca feels a sense of doom, knowing that whatever it is that moves so silently will surely kill it.

Then a diamond-shaped head arises, hesitates for a moment before it resumes its tracking, looking for a meal. It is a moment too long. I begin my flight downward, faster and faster, my eyes fixed on the colorful skin of the snake, which is now free of the tall grass.

My downward flight turns into a dive as I fold my wings. I am a streak across the gray Andes skies. I am a black dart screaming to the earth. I am death.

And now I strike. My talons just behind the head, crushing the flesh within them. I lift my wings and rise as the snake thrashes wildly, its tail swinging around my legs. I strike the head, pulling the flesh away from the small skull.

We go up and down, no higher than the height of the paca that stands transfixed against the high grass. I tear away more flesh, this time from the eyes.

This time from the skull that breaks beneath my beak.

The grip around my talons eases. It is over. I have my meal.

All is well.

I am living on the dark side of the moon. Pretending to be in another place, sometimes another time, and always in another light, I walk among my friends and the people I know as if everything is as it should be. Nothing is as it should be.

One of the things that scare me, that wake me up

in the middle of the night, is that I am too conscious of my thoughts. It's as if there is a talk show in my head that I'm constantly watching. I wonder if everyone has a talk show in their head. Or if they have voices laying out their future.

Never mind my address. Never mind that my mail comes to 145th Street, or that I live in a place called Harlem. It is really the dark side of the moon. In the mornings, I walk past guys a little older than I am. They stand on street corners or fill up the old gray stoops on my block and watch the world go by.

"They're not smart," Twig said when I mentioned them. "Half of them didn't even finish high school."

What I know is that it doesn't matter if they did or didn't finish. High school doesn't mean anything anymore. If you want to invent your own life, you need to have more than a high school diploma.

The school I go to, Phoenix, is the old Powell School at 128th and Amsterdam Avenue in Harlem. Red bricks are piled on top of red bricks to make an old New York building. Behind us, on what was once called Old Broadway, an overhead train whines and creaks its way through Harlem. A short distance away, the

George Bruce branch of the New York Public Library squats like a homeless woman with many stories to tell and few ears to give them to.

The library is where I live, really live. On 145th Street, I eat and sleep and go to the toilet, but it is only in that library, among the books, that I feel comfortable. I go inside, climb the steep steps, find a book, and lose myself for hours. I feel safe—as when I imagine myself flying over the square and rectangular Harlem rooftops, a predator looking for something evil to consume. But if the demons have been too much with me, even the books can't shelter me completely and I stop my reading to fight against them. It is always the same fight: I am the predator, they are the lowly tormentors, and in the end, I destroy them.

Sitting in Mr. Ramey's office, knowing what he was going to say long before the words fell between us, I could feel my balls shrivel up and my throat go dry. I wanted to plead my case to him, to say that if I didn't get a scholarship, it would mean taking my place with all the other guys on the block who look like me. Young, black, dangerous unless proven otherwise.

Twig rarely reads. But he told me that when the demons bother him, he puts them on a track. He watches them run ahead of him and then slowly and surely runs them down, catches up with them, and then speeds past, imagining how they feel knowing that they are losers. I think Twig is at his best when he is running, when he is dreaming of being in races, when he dreams of winning, when he dreams of holding a trophy above his head.

In a sane world, we would be heroes. Teachers would applaud as we walked into the school. There is the smart one, the one who wants to be a writer. And there is the runner.

But we have enemies. In our separate ways, we have moved away from the mob. They have settled for less and we are still hoping to be more. We haven't created a huge space, and we haven't escaped the huge shadow they cast. Our scent is no different from theirs, but we have separated ourselves. I think Twig is on the brink of being a great runner. One day, I hope, I will write a poem, or an essay, or a novel, that will change hearts. But the mob doesn't want us to be different. They want us to find our spots on the corner, or on a stoop. They beckon to us and tell us that everything will be okay.

But I'm terrified to be like them, to drift off into a

world that is so unreal. I watched too many times as my father slurred his words and mumbled about the life he had once hoped for. I see my mom sitting in the darkness wondering what has gone wrong with her life.

"You've got a good head on your shoulders, Darius," Mr. Ramey said. "But you haven't really been doing the work, have you?"

I didn't answer. What did he want, an admission? Should I have bowed my head and said, "Oh, I know I don't deserve anything, sir"?

"And why do you have to go away to college?" he went on. "You could work during the day and go to school at night for a while."

"No," I wanted to say. "I can't take care of myself and my mother and my brother and still wrap my head around the books. I'm not that strong. The only thing I have is a mind, and some writing ability. Shouldn't that be enough?"

When I left Mr. Ramey's office, I saw Midnight and Tall Boy down the hall. Put faces to my misery and they would have them.

Midnight, from his incredibly stupid heart to his heavy-legged walk, more stumble than stride, is garbage. He is slow, mean, a bully. If he can make anyone's life miserable, even for a few minutes, he jumps at the chance. The teachers hate him but give him as much room as they can so they don't have to deal with him. They look away when he hits a smaller kid in the hallway or takes someone's money. His eyes, almost the same color as his skin, make him look like a child's drawing of a "brown" teenager.

Tall Boy is his homey. Dull-faced, slow, with light, mottled skin that looks like he might have some kind of sickness, he has only his record of being in juvenile detention to brag about.

"I been in jail in Jersey City, *and* in the Bronx!"

Idiots don't know they're idiots, which is unfortunate.

Tall Boy is crappy, a follower, but nobody is as much of a shithead as Midnight.

The bell rang and the juniors were going to have an assembly. The auditorium was noisy as we shuffled in. I didn't want to sit with Twig because I felt so bad, so close to crying. I sat a few rows behind him.

I watched as Midnight and Tall Boy looked around for a place and then settled behind Twig. We had just finished saying the Pledge of Allegiance when

Midnight started kicking the back of Twig's chair. I knew he would do it all through the assembly. Twig turned once and Midnight mean mugged him. That's the kind of stuff he does. Just bother people. Just add some annoyance to another person's life. Just remind Twig that there's nothing he can do about it.

Midnight's name is Ronald Brown. He calls himself Midnight because, he says, that's when they execute people on death row. You're supposed to fall out over that little piece of crap. I didn't fall out.

Tall Boy's real name is Lawrence Lester. He's a fairly good basketball player but doesn't have the discipline to play on a team. Everybody keeps talking about how much potential he has, but I don't think he has anything going on except a lousy attitude.

Both of them add up to nothing.

Twig's real name is Manuel Fernandez, but his grandfather gave him the nickname Twig. When we were in the fourth grade, Twig and I discovered that we did stuff. A lot of people do one thing or another, but Twig was interesting because he did a *lot* of stuff. We both played ball, he liked to draw, I liked writing, and we both tried out for the tennis team. Twig made the team and I didn't, but I practiced with him. We were nine when we met and now we're both sixteen and we're still best friends.

Twig can run. He isn't much of a sprinter, but he started running the 800 in middle school and moved up to the mile and cross-country in high school. He can run really long distances, and over the summer he ran an open cross-country race against people of all ages. He came in third even though some of the men in the race were in college. Mr. Day, Phoenix's track coach, was knocked out by Twig's running and asked him to join the track team. They were going to mention him at the assembly, and I was happy about that.

"Before I begin talking about our expectations for the new year," Mrs. Nixon, our principal, started, "I would like Mr. Day, our athletic director, to say a few words."

Mr. Day was about fifty, balding, and walked with his shoulders hunched. He was supposed to be half black and half white, but he just talked and acted like a black dude. He came out and started talking about how good the Frederick Douglass Academy teams were and everybody started booing. Frederick Douglass Academy, or FDA, was our biggest rival in just about everything. The fact was, they had got some kind of athletic grant from the city and thought they were special. Anyway, after the booing died down, Mr. Day spoke.

"We've always done well against FDA in track and field," he said. "We were always neck and neck with them in total point scores, but in the years we were edged out, it was always in the distance races. This year, we are adding a very good young distance runner to our squad, Manuel Fernandez. Manuel, please stand up."

Twig stood up and almost everybody gave him a hand. Everybody but Midnight and Tall Boy. Both of them put their hands over their mouths and laughed.

Why does laughing replace so much for some people? If something wasn't funny, why were they laughing? It was as if they could somehow make things less important, or people less important, by just laughing at them. Could I write a poem about Tall Boy? How would I avoid the clichés? How would I avoid such adjectives as *stupid* and *gross*? What could I say on Tall Boy's level that he would understand?

When Twig sat down, Midnight started kicking the back of his chair again. It really made me mad, but

I knew I couldn't beat Midnight in a fight. Neither could Twig.

Mrs. Nixon's talk was all right—how she expected each of us to do our best and how she knew how good our best was. I was just happy with Mr. Day for having Twig stand up.

If you knew Twig, you would like him. Even if you just met him, you would think he was okay. He looks like an average kid until he smiles, and then his whole face lights up and you just want to smile with him. Twig is two inches shorter than me. He's five eight and a half and I'm five ten and a half. He's thin, with light tan skin, dark hair and eyes, and a wide smile that makes him seem always pleased with something. My mom says he would have made a pretty girl. He told me that when he was born, he was premature.

"My mom said she was expecting me in October and I came along in August," he said. "I guess I couldn't wait."

"You didn't have anything to do with it," I said. "It's like . . . nature or something."

"Too many people are born in October, anyway," Twig said. "You don't hear about a lot of people being born in August."

"I saw Midnight and Tall Boy kicking your chair in assembly," I said.

"They don't bother me." Twig's voice was low as he looked away.

"They bother me," I said.

"Yeah, they're like a blister on your foot," he said. "Even if they don't hurt when you start a race, you know that sooner or later they're going to show up."

chapter three

Peregrines hunt live birds, diving from great heights to strike prey with their talons. Sometimes the peregrine bites the neck of its victim to ensure death. Although usually found in the wild, many peregrines now live in cities.

"So what we need to do," Twig said, "is get Midnight and Tall Boy outside in the playground and have a shootout. We'll be space invaders or something, and we'll challenge them to a duel."

"I'll shoot Midnight first," I said. "And then Tall Boy will panic and start moving away."

"Right," Twig said, "and then I'll shoot Tall Boy in his knees and he'll fall to the ground. But first you see his shadow kind of folding up, and then you see him reaching for his knees as he falls."

"Yeah, he's in a lot of pain, but he thinks he's going to make it," I said. "He's figuring out how to make a comeback, but then, way up on the top of a tree, *Fury* sees him.

"That's the name I'm going to give my peregrine falcon," I said. "I like that name. There's a lot of *emotion* in it."

"*Fury* with cold eyes and talons of steel!" Twig said.

"With no mercy in his heart!" I said.

"He swoops down and snatches out Midnight's eyeballs in one pass!"

"Midnight's blind and reaching around for something to hold on to, but he finds nothing," I said.

"Did you see he pushed something down the back of my collar today?" Twig asked.

"What?"

Twig took a small piece of paper from his pocket and showed it to me. It had one word on it: *Faggot!*

chapter four

The falcon rests.

"Aunt Dotty was over." My eleven-year-old brother, Brian, was lying on his stomach across the bed, moving checkers on the board on the floor.

"What did she want?"

"To see me," he said. "She had some money to give me."

"She gave you some money?"

"That's private information." He pushed a checker across the board with his forefinger.

"If she gave you money, then she must have left some for me, too," I said. "She doesn't just give one of us money."

"What you need money for?"

I went over to the bed and sat on him.

"Get up, Darius." Brian started trying to push me off. "You could kill me like this!"

"How?" I asked, bouncing.

"You could bust my heart, man!"

"How much did Aunt Dot give you?" I asked.

"Ten dollars, fool—now get off of me!"

"So I'm supposed to get five, right?"

"You were, but I spent it." Brian rolled over, holding his chest. "I needed some oil sticks."

"And you spent the whole ten dollars on your art supplies?"

"No, I only spent five, but then I noticed it was *your* five."

I jumped on him again and started bouncing on his back.

The thing with Brian is that he likes to wrestle around but sometimes he gets too much into it and then he starts to cry and Mama gets mad at me. She knows I probably didn't hurt the tadpole, but she just gets upset if one of us cries.

I finally got my brother to rescue my five dollars from his closet and hand it over. Then I wondered if there had been more money.

"If Aunt Dot left more than five for me, I will personally snatch your heart out of your chubby brown body and beat it with a hammer."

"You want to go to Mickey D's?" Brian asked.

"No, I'm going downtown with Twig," I said. "He's going to run all the way from 59th to 110th Street."

"I can do that," he said. "If I didn't have to wait for Mama to get home, I'd go with you guys and beat both of you uptown."

"You couldn't beat your shadow if you were running toward the sun," I said.

"What's that mean?" he asked.

"Figure it out," I answered.

I took my bike out of the corner of the kitchen, where my uncle Jimmy had put up a hook that kept it off the floor. "Tell Mama I won't be late," I said.

"She said *she* was going to be late," Brian said. He was looking under the cushions on the sofa, probably for the remote. "Home Depot is having an inventory night. Or maybe it was an inventory sale—I don't know, something. Tell Twig I said hello and that I could beat him any day of the week."

I hoped she wasn't going to lose another job.

As I locked the door, I thought about Brian racing Twig. Brian couldn't beat anybody running. My brother is just barely five foot five without shoes, with short little legs and toes that point out when he walks. I even started calling him the Penguin for a while, but Mama said it made him feel bad. There are a lot of things in our family that I think could make him feel bad, especially her drinking and crying jags, but I don't say anything to her about it. He spends too much time by himself playing video games, I know.

Brian said he wouldn't have left if he had been our father.

"What would you do?" I asked.

He managed a shrug.

I met Twig on the corner and we walked up the hill to the A train on 145th. Twig had on his sweats and his practice running shoes.

"Don't tell me you kids are going to no school with a bicycle!" The clerk at the 145th Street station was short, squat, and mean looking. I think she was born that way, because I can't imagine her ever working up a smile.

"This is an after-school program at the Schomburg on 135th Street," I said. "We have to be there."

She turned her mean face into something even

meaner and motioned toward the gate.

"It's getting too expensive to live in New York," I said to Twig when we had gotten on the train. "I'm thinking of moving to Colorado."

"Colorado?" Twig leaned back from me. "What are you going to do in Colorado? All they have there is a lot of snow, a lot of mountains, and the dumbbutt Broncos. You like the Broncos?"

"Not really," I said. "But my mother said that in two years or so, New York will cost too much for people like us. Then maybe they'll have to move everybody out to Colorado."

"If you get to be a famous writer or a poet, Colorado might be okay," Twig said. "That's *if* they got black poets out there. I never heard of a black poet who lived in Colorado."

"Twig, they have black people everywhere."

"Then how come none of the blacks who play for the Broncos are from around there?" he asked. "They're all from Georgia and Arkansas and places like that."

We got off at 59th Street and Central Park West and Twig started stretching.

"What time you going for?" I asked.

"Twenty-five minutes," Twig said, bringing his

right heel back to the top of his butt. "It's going to be hard if there are a lot of kids in the way, especially around 84th Street."

"You saving your new shoes for official races?" I asked, noticing he had on his old Nikes.

"They got cleats for dirt tracks," Twig said. He spread his legs slightly and touched both palms to the ground.

"What's that supposed to do?" I asked.

"I don't know, but it looks cool, right?"

Twig was running and I was riding behind him. I imagined him thinking about me, wondering how close, wondering what I was thinking. I was looking at my watch, trying to figure out times. This was an easy run for him, and he moved swiftly past the park benches and the black women pushing small white children along the park's edge. There was no wasted movement with Twig. His stride wasn't that long, and his thin arms barely moved as we went block after block. The people watching him knew that he was in training. I thought they were connected to him for a brief moment. As I was connected with him.

For a minute I felt a sense of disappointment. I knew Twig would run and become someone who would be at least a footnote to the history of our school. Some people will make a mark, a footnote, and others will disappear without a trace. Mr. Ramey's comments about my grades came to me again. He was talking about my chances of getting a scholarship, but we both knew it was also about my whole life. Maybe one day I'd disappear.

I thought of my father telling us how he used to go over to 126th Street in the mornings and stand on the corner, waiting for the trucks to come by that would pick up workers for the day. I knew they paid him whatever they wanted, and that he would pretend to be happy with it.

"You know, that's what being a man is all about," he would say when he came home.

I didn't think that was what made a man. Or that a man needed to be made once he was born.

My mother says she doesn't think of her husband. Right. Like Twig doesn't think about Midnight.

chapter five

The Writers' Workshop. Miss Carroll stood near the window, as nervous as usual. She put her thin white hand across her chest and touched her left shoulder. I knew she would do it twenty times and the class only lasted forty-five minutes.

"Great fiction demands that you allow your reader into the story as spectator and creator," she said. "The reader wants this involvement, and the more you allow her in, the more rewarding the story will be."

"But you're always saying be specific," Essie said. "So if someone picks up 'stuff' around a room, you're sticking little notes in the margins saying 'What stuff?' Why not let the reader figure it out?"

"Because the 'stuff' around the room is not what

your story is about and doesn't give any flesh to the story," Miss Carroll said. "That's why you skimmed over it in the first place."

I like Miss Carroll, even if she is sometimes almost too jumpy to be around. There is something other-worldly about her, maybe even other-weirdly. She told the class once that when she was very young, she used to cut her arms. It was too much for us to hear, and too hard to deal with, so nobody in the class made a comment. But I like her because she says good things about my writing, although she said once that I often put my intellect between me and the reader. For her to actually *know* that, she would have to know much more about me than she does. Who am I except my intellect?

The story that came back from the *Delta Review* had a short note handwritten on a paper with their letterhead on it. It read:

Dear Darius Austin:
   We liked "The Song of a Thousand Dolphins" very much and would like to reconsider it. What made it a near miss and not an acceptance is that we were not sure if the boy was trusting

the dolphins or if he was actually waiting for them to fail and, thus, was taking his own life. If he was trusting the dolphins to keep him safe, we would like to make that clearer and would love to see the story again.

Lionel Dornich

The story was about a ten-year-old boy with a bad leg who lived in an orphanage near a beach. One day he swam out too far toward a small island and, nearly exhausted, was nudged back toward the shore by a dolphin. After that he would swim out great distances from the shore, pushing himself more and more until he was exhausted, and then would again be pushed back by one or more dolphins. I had ended the story with his last swim, leaving the possibility that he might actually reach the island, or he might perish if the dolphins didn't rescue him.

But in my mind I didn't know what was in the boy's thoughts. I didn't know if he was ready to give up or if he trusted the dolphins. I wanted to revise the story to get it published, but I wasn't sure if I could convince an editor if I wasn't sure myself.

I showed Miss Carroll the note but not the story.

She lifted the small sheet of paper and looked under it as if she were looking for the story.

"We're always too careful about revealing ourselves," she said.

I wanted to show the story to Miss Carroll, but I knew that it was probably my most successful story and that I would be crushed if she didn't like it.

I feel a bond with her and what she knows about writing. She picks up a poem and it comes alive in her weak, quavering voice. She reads a play and talks about it in a way that lights the stage, that makes it so real you feel you have always known the characters, that you just haven't noticed them so close to you.

I think she is going to turn me into the writer I want to be, the one who Twig says I already am.

Chapter Six

"So, who's rich?" I asked when I saw Brian sitting on the steps.

"Who?"

"Me."

"You got your bookie money?" he guessed correctly.

"The reading money, yeah."

"They shouldn't have that just for juniors," my brother complained. "It's not fair."

"It's not supposed to be fair," I said. "It's an experiment. Juniors are responsible, so you can see what will happen. Eleven-year-olds are flaky."

"If you gave me ten dollars a book, I'd read night and day!" Brian looked at me sideways. "You get to read a book a week and they pay you because you're a junior, and all it means is that you want some money."

"In the first place there wouldn't be any reason for you to read night and day, because you can only get money for one book a week, so that's forty books a school year," I reminded him. "And they tried it two years ago with grade school kids, and what happened?"

"I don't care what happened two years ago," Brian said. "This is *this* year!"

"I'm thinking about buying some Chinese food," I said. I walked past him into the building.

"I want shrimp fried rice," he said, following me into the hallway. "And egg rolls."

"What makes you think I'm getting anything for you?"

"Mama is not going to let you buy food for you and not get anything for me, and you know it, D-Boy."

"She doesn't know I got the reading money."

"No, but you're going to tell her like you always do, and she's going to smile and tell you how proud she is of you, and then you're going to play big-time and tell us what you're going to do with the money. Right?"

"Yep. And I'm glad it's not fair."

The electric company came up with the idea of

paying kids to read books. You could read one book a week from the school list, four books a month, then prove you really understood the books by taking a test at the end of the month. If you passed the test, you got ten dollars for each book you read. To me, it was a way of making a few extra dollars, and I liked most of the books on the list. During the past month, I had read Anne Frank's *The Diary of a Young Girl*, *A Separate Peace*, *Dragonwings*, and *The Red Badge of Courage*.

"You think Mama is going to want Chinese food?" Brian asked.

"Probably," I answered.

"Bet she wants beef with snow peas," he said as we reached the door.

I unlocked the door and Brian pushed past me— I knew he would because that's the sort of immature kid he is—and announced that I had what he called my *bookie* money.

"Brian, go in the bathroom and get me a washcloth from under the sink," Mama's voice came from somewhere.

"Where are you?" Brian asked.

"Under the sink in the kitchen!" she called. "Will you get me the washcloth, boy?"

Brian looked under the kitchen table toward the sink as I walked around it. Mama's legs were sticking out, and there were a screwdriver and a wrench next to her.

"What are you doing?" I asked.

"The drain is stopped up," she said. "I got the nut off the trap, but I can't get to whatever is in there."

"You want me to try?"

"No."

"Why don't you call the landlord?"

"Because I don't want to hear his mouth talking about when are we going to get the rent to him," Mama answered. I could hear the strain in her voice, and I saw that the back of her hand was scraped and bleeding.

"I'll try to get it out," I said.

She pulled herself from under the sink as Brian came in with the washcloth. Mama took it from him and held it against her scraped hand. She sat up, and for a moment I thought she was going to cry.

"I've been trying to unstick it with a hanger," she said. "If I can't get it with the hanger, maybe I'll buy a little snake at work. That's another ten dollars!"

"Why don't you let me try it?" I said.

"Change your clothes first," she said. "No use messing up your school clothes."

"Darius got his money for reading books," Brian said.

"You've said that, Brian!"

"Yes, ma'am." My brother glanced at me and turned away.

I went to my room and quickly changed into my jeans. I hung my shirt up on a nail in the closet and then came back.

"She got it open!" Brian announced.

"Who put paper in the damn sink?" she asked.

I figured it had to be either me or Brian, but neither of us said anything. When I saw that the paper was from a magazine, I knew it was my brother.

Mama had let the water run into a bucket, and I took it into the bathroom and emptied it down the toilet. The paper went into the toilet, too, and I reached in and grabbed it before it went down. When I got back into the kitchen, Mom was struggling with the wrench.

"I'll do that," I said.

"It's tight enough," she said. "Just check it once in a while to make sure it's not leaking."

"Yes, ma'am."

I helped her off the floor. She looked at her hands and arms, streaked with dirt, dark except where she had scraped away some skin, and started toward the bathroom.

"Darius, the gas didn't light and I used a magazine page to light it," Brian whispered.

"One page?"

"Maybe a couple," Brian said. "You think I should say something?"

"No, just tell yourself how stupid you are."

Mama was in the bathroom awhile, and when she came out I could smell alcohol on her breath. I asked her if she was okay, and she nodded.

"There's leftover beef stew in the refrigerator," she said. "You guys want that? I'm going to have to change and get out of here."

"Yeah, that's fine," I said. "How come the rent isn't paid?"

"Because I forgot it! Okay? I forgot it!" Mama's voice filled our small kitchen.

She sat, elbows on the table, her head forward in her hands. Neither Brian nor I wanted to say anything else, and we just sat there in the silence. The refrigerator hummed and clicked in the corner. From the alley behind the house, a dog's bark announced he was there.

"I didn't forget the rent," she said after a while. "I forgot the electric bill, and then when I went to pay it, I saw that it was more than I thought it would be. They laid some people off at the job, and I thought the rest of us were going to get some overtime, but . . . it just didn't happen."

"I got forty dollars," I said.

"We'll be straight by the end of the month," Mama said. "There's just an extra week or something in this month."

She smiled.

I put the beef stew on when Mama had left for her job at Home Depot. It had been good the night before and it would be all right again.

"I messed up, right?" Brian said.

"No, you're straight. She's just upset because they cut a day out of her job," I said. "She was working four days and now she's working three. That's what's messed up. That's like twenty-five percent of your income gone. We were just sliding by before that."

I don't remember us ever doing all that great. Maybe we were at one time, but I can't remember it.

Mama has told Brian and me stories about when she and my father first married.

"We were married at the Church of the Master on Morningside Avenue," she said. "When we left the church, the limousine took us right to my mother's house and waited for us to change clothes. Then we went to the airport and flew to Bermuda for our honeymoon. It was as if we were in a magazine or something."

She told us how they struggled with two small kids and how my father joined the National Guard for the extra money. Then he went to Iraq.

"When he came back, he was missing something," she told us, holding his picture in his desert camouflage uniform. "He lost a lot of weight and was always off in a fog. I knew he was messing with drugs, but I thought we could work our way through it. He drifted further and further away, and then one day, he said he had to leave before he killed somebody."

"And he left?"

"Yeah, he just left," she said. "But he keeps us in whatever piece of mind he still has. I know that."

I don't know it.

chapter seven

Van Cortlandt Park was filled with brown, black, and white people moving along the paths, their bright colors looking even more brilliant in the sharp autumn sunlight. A group of kids were making swishing noises through the piled leaves beneath the trees. Some Latina women sat on the benches across from the handball courts. And there were little kids everywhere. When our track team got off the bus, some of the kids stopped for a moment to watch them.

The whole team went through their fifteen minutes of stretching, then fifteen minutes of warm-up exercises, and then broke off into their individual training. The middle- and long-distance runners were to do a thirty-minute run through the park, walk for five minutes, and then do another thirty-minute run.

After the first thirty-minute run, when the distance runners were walking, Mr. Day came up to me.

"You need to keep an eye on your boy Fernandez," he said, sitting on the bench next to me. "Sometimes guys with South American and Mexican backgrounds don't like to train. They see they're on the team and all they want to do is show off their uniforms to *las chicas*."

"Oh, yeah?" I said. *Bullshit*, I thought.

The sprinters were the stars of the track team, and they got all the attention. Some of the sprinters would go on to college and be on track teams there; others were football players or baseball players who just used track to keep in shape for their other sports. I knew Twig didn't think the cross-country guys got enough training, so he worked out on his own as much as he could.

"You got to help me train," he had said. "When we have a meet and some guy thinks he's just going to run away with everything, I want to ease on by him at the start of the last half mile and just leave him in the dust."

I had thought I knew Twig when he ran earlier, but after I laid out a plan for him, he really got serious with it. We had found an article about how this older runner, a guy named Ted Corbitt, had trained by running seven miles to work every morning and then running home at night. Twig said he wanted to run twenty-five miles a week, and I made up a schedule for him.

Practice was over in three hours and Twig and I got our backpacks from the bus. He said he wanted to do some sprints.

"Why?"

"Say the race is between me and some dude and we're running right next to each other at the top of the home stretch. We both see it's like sixty-five yards to go, which is like a heartbeat. He wants to win and I want to win, so it's tear up the friggin' track and whoever gets across the line first wins it! I know if I practice sprints and he doesn't, then it's going to be me."

"Is that what you're thinking when you're running?" I asked.

"No, man, that's what I'm thinking when I'm figuring out how a race might go." Twig had his legs straight in front of him and crossed at the ankle.

"When I'm racing, I know it's going to start hurting somewhere along the line. My legs are going to hurt and my lungs are going to be burning. But that's when I know I have to keep pushing it. I can't give in. When I'm practicing, I know it's not what's really going down because you don't practice that hard. At least we don't. But I have to get myself mentally ready for when it gets hard, when it hurts."

"You don't think about just beating somebody?"

"My grandmother says that there's only one person to beat," Twig said. "That's yourself. If you don't beat yourself, it's going to be hard for anybody else to beat you."

"Your grandmother is into racing?"

"No, she's into *me*, man." Twig smiled.

Twig walked out onto the track and lined up at the hundred-yard marker. My watch had a second hand and I tried to keep an eye on it and on Twig at the same time. When he took off, he stumbled a bit but still got the hundred in under eleven seconds.

The next two times, he got almost exactly eleven.

The last two were a little over twelve. If he could do that in a race at the end of a 3K, he would be hard to beat.

Twig went to the men's room and then put his sweats over his practice track suit. We walked out of the park and got the bus downtown to Harlem. There were some Latina girls on the bus, and two of them started looking toward us and giggling. Two Muslim girls, also in Catholic school uniforms but wearing hijabs, came on and sat across from us.

"Do you know why those girls like me?" Twig asked.

"They're looking at me," I said. "Girls always go for good-looking guys."

"No, man, they see me and they know I'm Dominican and all Dominicans can dance!"

"You can dance?"

"I'm not great," Twig said. "But I can dance."

"You get on the floor and wait for the pain to come?" I asked. "And then you dance through it?"

"Darius, that is funny! If my mind was as fast as yours, you know, if I could think of funny things to say like that . . . I'd have to get pepper spray to beat the girls off!"

When the guys in the hoodies first got on, I thought it was Tall Boy and another kid from our school. It wasn't. Just two guys with their pants hanging down, being stupid. They sat diagonally from the two girls in hijabs and started pointing and laughing at them. The two girls were embarrassed. Both of them put their heads down.

An older man, a white guy with white hair over his temples and a red, splotched forehead, spoke up. "These are good young girls," he said. "Why don't you leave them alone!"

Both of the hoodies laughed as if it were the funniest thing they had ever heard.

"Keep it down back there." This from the bus driver.

"Why don't you go and die, old man?" From one of the hoodies.

"We'll all die one day," the old man, his face turning redder, said. "Might as well live decently in the meanwhile."

The bus came to a stop and the hoodies got up to leave. One stood in the doorway and held it open while the other one confronted the white man.

"Guess what, punk!" The hoodie leaned over the old man, his face inches from him. "I don't give a fuck!"

He drew back a fist and then broke out into a high laugh when the man flinched.

After the two hoodies got off the bus, there was a moment of silence. We were all relieved.

"I feel stupid for not saying something," Twig said as we got off the bus at 145th Street. "I should have said something to those guys."

"And get beat up?" I asked. "Stabbed or something?"

"You didn't feel like that?"

"Yeah, I did. They took something from everyone on the friggin' bus," I said. "It's like they had all the power and we didn't have anything. People like that I would like to—"

Twig put his fingertips in front of my mouth. "Darius, don't go dark on me," he said. "I think you're going dark."

"What do you mean?"

"I mean if you think about doing things to people like that, if you think about it too much, it gets all up in you and you can't control it after a while. Then they really got you."

"Whatever."

"No, really, man. Really."

I thought about the falcon, his gray body almost invisible as he watched the streets from his nest just below the rooftop. His mind wasn't dark. He knew what he had to do, what he was about.

chapter eight

Fury sits on my wrist, and I can feel the power of his talons as he grips the thick leather glove. I am breathing hard but he barely moves, only rocking slightly as he anticipates the hunt. I reach for the string that covers his mask, and taking the other string in my teeth, I loosen it. He turns his head quickly and sees it is me.

We are not friends. He is not my pet. We are hunters. I loosen the cord around his feet and feel the tension easing and tightening on my hand as he waits for the signal. I lift my wrist slightly, feeling his power as he shifts position. He flaps his wings but does not move from my arm.

Then I raise my wrist and arm again. It is his signal, and he lifts off in a great flurry of motion and climbs incredibly high in seconds. Now he is a dark silhouette against the blue-gray sky. Now, as he turns, the sun catches the brown ruffled feathers of his chest.

Below him, in the high grass swaying in the October breeze, a hoodie cackles and chases a squirrel, putting himself between the furry creature and the tree that is its home. The hoodie cackles again as the squirrel's small body shakes with fear.

Above, Fury glides in a huge circle, turns his body at a forty-five-degree angle, and begins his dive.

Twig is wrong, I'm not going dark. Sometimes I know my thoughts push in on me, and I want to push the pain out of my head. At times, I feel my anger rising—no, not my anger, my frustration. It rises like the stink from a sewer, useless, filling me with disgust for who I am.

There are moments when my thoughts just fill my head, like the white peanuts they use for packing boxes, and there's no room for anything besides the competition between what I hope will be my reality and the picture that people like Midnight and Tall Boy keep pushing into my consciousness.

If I told Twig what I saw in my future, he might understand, but he might not. And if he didn't understand, I'd be devastated.

"Twig," I would say, "I will be a famous writer one day. People on boats and subways and planes will read my books, and their heads, filled with my words, will be transported to other, very special places."

"I can dig it," he would answer.

"But what if Midnight is right about me?"

"No," Twig would protest. "He's nothing! Get him out of your mind, Darius."

But I know I won't be able to get Midnight out of my mind. What I know is that Midnight, stupid damn Midnight, has done all the math, checked the odds against me, fed them into his computer, and come up with a conclusion. In the talk show of my mind, I am telling myself that I can be anything I want to be, but my voice sounds whiny, hollow. I want to believe in the mantra that being poor doesn't matter and being black doesn't matter, but there are reminders that both matter very much.

The stairway. Between social studies and math, third and fourth period. Me going up, Midnight and Tall Boy coming down.

"Yo, Darius, I heard you joined the Latin Kings." This from Tall Boy.

"I didn't join anything," I said.

He shoved me toward the wall and put his knee

against my hip. It was an awkward position, and I thought I could get him away from me and down the stairs. But my heart was beating fast and my mouth went dry. I was afraid.

"Why don't you loan me one of those dollars you got in your pocket?" Tall Boy said.

"He's probably got a welfare food card, too," Midnight said, smirking.

I tried to slide past and Tall Boy leaned on me, pinning me against the wall. Again he lifted his knee and tried to dig it into my chest. Bending my knees, I grabbed his other leg and lifted it, and suddenly he was scrambling to keep his balance.

I could have thrown him down the stairs, let him know I wasn't afraid of him, that I was strong. Instead I put his knee down and twisted away.

Midnight punched at me, hitting me in the shoulder, and I swung back as hard as I could. The blow landed high on his head, and for a moment, the two of them were in a scramble to get their footing as I went past them and up the stairs. Then Tall Boy was after me. He caught me on the landing and swung his fist from behind. I felt the punches but they didn't hurt. Tall Boy clamped his arm around my neck and shoved his hand into my pocket.

"What's going on?" A woman's voice.

"He tried to steal my money," I heard Tall Boy saying. "But I got it!"

Midnight and Tall Boy started down the stairs again.

"Why are you boys always fighting?" The teacher's voice.

I looked up and saw Miss Carroll. She knows better. We all do.

There are reminders.

Mom and Brian and me are at the rental office, seated on the light wooden benches with their green-and-yellow cushions that pretend to be artistic. Mom is sitting next to me, the anxiety scribbled across her face. Brian, feeling on display, fidgets by her other side. All I can think of is what happened today in school.

"The key, Mrs. Austin, is financial stability. That's the new buzzword in the rental and sale aspects of housing. Quite frankly, we don't know where the market is going. . . ."

"I thought the city paid part of the rent," Mom says. "That these apartments were part of a program—"

"That pays part of the rental fees, as you say," the agent goes on. "But there are minimum incomes required as a means to keep the apartments stable and on the market. . . ."

The rental agent drones on and on. But the tone says enough, the words don't matter, we won't get the apartment Mom has applied for. Even though she has prayed over it, even though she has costumed herself in her best dress and smeared shea butter over Brian's face, and has straightened the tie she asked me to wear, we won't be getting a new apartment.

Why don't people understand that the words don't matter? Why do they fill their mouths with syllables when the words never mean anything? If they say them softly (*Why are you boys always fighting?*) or if they shout them (*I DON'T GIVE A FUCK!*), they are empty.

Mom is quiet on the way home, but I know she is hurting. That's one thing we learn to be good at, be quiet when we are hurt.

I think of doing something to the rental agent, as if anything were his fault alone. It's not, but I still think of doing something to him. I imagine Fury, his dark feathers like a black cape of darkness, my alter ego, predator. Twig thinks I am growing dark and he is right. He wants me to live through the pain. I don't think I can.

chapter nine

"Mama, what's a prose?" Brian was smearing butter on his toast.

"Don't start it, birdbrain!" I said.

"What's *what*?" Mama asked.

"A *prose*." Brian looked over at me. "Darius said he was writing a poem, but I thought he was writing a prose, and then he said there was nothing called a prose."

"Prose is like . . . when it's not poetry," Mama said. "It doesn't rhyme or anything."

"That's what I told him, but he said I was wrong." Brian wiggled his shoulders the way he always does when he's feeling smug.

"Poetry doesn't have to rhyme," I said. "*Some* poetry rhymes and *some* doesn't."

"How are you going to tell a poem from a prose if it doesn't rhyme?" Brian was into his argument and feeling confident. "If it don't rhyme, the poem's a crime."

"Brian, why are you so stupid in the mornings?" I asked.

"He's not stupid," Mama said. "He's just . . ."

I gave it a minute before I said, "I agree!"

"She didn't say anything!" Brian said.

"Will you two quit it!" Mama said. "Look, it's almost time for you to go to school. Let's say a quick prayer, and then off you go."

"Is something wrong?" I asked.

"Like *what*?" Mom asked.

"'Cause we're praying and it's not even Sunday," Brian said.

"Have we slipped that far from God?" Mama asked, holding out her hands to us.

Brian took Mama's hand, and she quickly moved it away and wiped the butter from her fingers. Then she bowed her head.

"Lord, look after my family today," she said. "Keep them safe and happy. In the name of the Father, the Son, and the Holy Ghost, amen."

Brian and I both said amens and then we started to get ourselves ready for school. We were just about out the door when Mom said there had been a call for me.

"Twig called last night," she said. "He sounded a little upset, but he said he was okay."

"You asked him if he was upset?"

"Yes, I asked him," Mom said. "I like that boy."

Brian goes to the Harlem School of the Arts and met up with two girls from his school on the corner. I told him I'd see him later.

"I'll write you another poem, before I come ho-em," he said.

I didn't find Twig until noon. He was sitting near the window in the lunchroom and I asked him what was up.

"I got something called broccoli and cheese casserole and it looks nasty," he said, pushing his lunch around on the plate.

"Why did you get it?"

"It sounds healthy," he said.

"If food doesn't look healthy, it's not healthy," I said. "That's direct from the Darius School of Nutrition!"

"What did you get?"

"Swiss steak, rice, and green beans," I said. "Now, that looks healthy."

"How's your story coming along?" Twig asked. "You started revising it yet?"

"Not yet," I answered.

"You remember that part where the kid is swimming out from the shore and there are clouds in the sky and you said—or the kid was thinking—that maybe the clouds were an omen?"

"Yeah?"

"What did you mean by that?"

I didn't expect Twig to bring up my story, or even to be thinking about it. "He hadn't seen any clouds when he was swimming on the other days," I said. "On that day he saw some black clouds and was thinking it might mean something. How come you're asking about the story?"

"I was talking to my uncle Ernesto yesterday." Twig's voice lowered. "He asked me to come into the kitchen and sit at the table with him, which right away is a bad sign. But then he was playing with a pencil, real casual like, you know, twisting it between his fingers, stuff like that. So I'm saying he's going to drop something on me. I could feel it. It was like an omen. And I thought about your story."

"He drop something on you?"

"He wants me to work in his bodega after school," Twig said. "He said I'm the oldest boy and he's thinking of leaving the bodega to me when he dies."

"He's going to pay you?"

"Twenty dollars a week. But I'll be like his slave," Twig said. "He'll be sitting on a crate of Corona and playing dominoes all day and I'll be hauling boxes around. No way."

"How old is he?"

"He's only thirty-three," Twig said. "He'll probably live until he's fifty-three or something. I don't want to work in no bodega for twenty years. And anyway, I can't be on the track team and work in the bodega the way he wants."

"You tell him that?"

"Yeah, but he doesn't care. And my mom is on the fence," Twig said. "She's talking about how family has to stick together and everything. Me being a slave is not about family sticking together."

"How about your grandmother?"

"She wants me to do what I want to do," Twig

said. "But it's my mom I'm worried about. She's, like, halfway between we have to do what my uncle says because he's family, and halfway between we're poor and it's a business, and halfway to wanting to see me happy."

"That's three halfways," I said.

"That's what we got," Twig said. "My grandmother, my mother, my uncle, and me. I don't want to go against my mom, though. That's why I thought you should come over to my uncle's bodega and say something."

"Me?" I asked. "Like *what*?"

"My mom likes you and my grandma likes you," Twig said. "And you talk really good, like you know something. They'll listen to you, man. You got to come up with something. Maybe come and see me run. That might be cool if I do all right."

"I'll come up with something," I said.

"Yo, Darius, can I ask you another question about your story?"

"Sure."

"In your story the kid is swimming, but he's got a messed-up leg so it's got to be hard for him, right?"

"Go on."

"Why did you give him a messed-up leg?" Twig asked. "Your legs are all right, aren't they?"

"I just did," I said. "No particular reason."

"Oh."

I watched as Twig walked down the hall to his next class, my stomach already churning.

chapter ten

Panic. My stomach turning, the palms of my hands growing clammy.

I didn't want Twig to have problems. I wanted him to find the races and run them and win them. I wanted it all to be simple for him even though it wasn't simple for me. What I wanted for my friend was a clear path around the track. What I wanted for me was a way through all the truths that people were laying on me.

Mr. Ramey was saying that my grades weren't good enough for a scholarship, and that was true in his world. But did he know what I could do, what I could accomplish?

Midnight was saying that I was too soft, too much

of a punk to make it in his world. And that was true, but did he know what I could do if I could get into my world? How far I could go?

The chorus in school was that if you did the right thing, that if you worked hard, you would succeed. And how many worlds was that true in? Was it true in my mother's world? Was it true in my father's world?

"You can be anything you want to be!" Not true. Did crackheads really want to be crackheads? Did homeless people really want to live on rooftops?

When he runs, it is only Twig. No one has to approve him, no one can dismiss what he accomplishes on the track. When the pain comes, he is ready to fight it, to overcome it.

What do I do when the pain comes?

chapter eleven

I had met Twig's uncle before. He is short, thin, and aggressive. He is the color of sand, except for his jaws, which are stubbly with a two-day beard. He leans back when he sees me so he can look down his nose. I have heard his stories about how he spent two years in the air force as a military policeman, and how he could disable a person in a flash, all told with a sinister stare and a snap of the fingers.

"What are you, Haitian?" he asked me, knowing I'm not Haitian.

"American," I answered.

"American." He said the word as if it were something vulgar, as if I were something vulgar.

Twig's mother and grandmother were at the

bodega as well. His grandmother sat on a cane chair with matching seat cushion and chair back cover.

Twig's mother sipped dark coffee from a cup.

"Black people think life is about being athletes," his uncle said. "They're not smart." He tapped his forefinger against the side of his skull to show where the brain was.

He had reminded me that I am black. Or, rather, he had reminded me that he considers me inferior.

"Everybody is smart," Twig's mother said.

"If he's smart, he can answer my questions," the uncle said. Then, turning to me and pointing one finger, he asked me again if I was smart.

"He's smart," Twig said.

"Then you tell me this, my smart friend." He crossed his arms over his chest and turned his head slightly sideways. Confident. "You go to school to get an education and then that's supposed to help you get a good job, right?"

"Yes," I said, knowing it was a trap.

"And if you are lucky, maybe you can get your own business and not have to work for somebody else for the rest of your life, right?"

"Could be," I said, feeling the noose tighten.

"It's not 'could be,'" he said. "It's either right or it's not right. Which is it? You're supposed to be smart."

"It's right," I said.

"So if you can get your own business when you are young, without wasting your time in college chasing Anglo girls, and you can get a good start in life, *and* you can help your family, that would be the best thing to do, right?"

"Depends on what the business is," I said. "If the business isn't good, you're better off going to college."

"Business isn't good or bad," his uncle said. "It's what you make it. If you're willing to work hard, it's good. If you're lazy, like some black people, then every business is bad."

"If Twig can go to college, he'll be better off than working in a bodega," I said. "You work in a bodega and you're not lazy and it's not much, right?"

"*Twig?* What kind of name is Twig? That's a black name. What you think is so smart is only smart for black people. So in your head, you think you got something. You got *nada*! Now it's time for you to leave, because you don't know anything."

"His father was Tree and so he is Twig," the mother said. "What do you have better than that? Eh?"

"Why don't you come and see him run one day?" I said, feeling defeated.

"Because I am a businessman," Twig's uncle said. "Businessmen don't take days away from their business to see some boys running around in short pants."

He turned away from me. Not halfway, but completely so that his back was to me, as if he had dismissed me entirely.

"Margarita, as the senior man in the family, as the patriarch, I am offering the boy a chance to do something with his life. If you are smart, you will tell him to take this offer. And it's up to you, of course, but I think you should not have him running around with Haitians. They're no good on the island, and they're no good here."

"Are you afraid to see how good Twig is?" I asked.

Slowly he turned to me. He looked me up and down. "Don't you ever say that I'm afraid of anybody! I could break you in a minute. Less than a minute! Do you hear that? Do you *hear* that?"

"Ernesto." Twig's grandmother spoke up. "He didn't ask you if you were afraid of him. He asked if you were afraid to see the boy run."

"Go outside," Twig's uncle said, smiling. "Run up and down the street. I'll watch you."

"Come see him race," Twig's mother said softly. "Then we'll decide."

"I'm not going to keep this job open forever," his uncle said. "By the time you race, it might be gone."

"You're afraid," I said. "You don't want to know how good he is."

He jumped from the stool and put his left hand against my right shoulder and pushed hard. As I turned, he got behind me and put his arm around my neck and pulled me back.

"Ernesto!" Twig's mother pushed her arms between us. "If this is how you treat young people, then I don't want my son anywhere near you!"

He held me for a moment longer, squeezing my neck so I would react.

"Yo, man, let him go!" Twig spoke up. "What's wrong with you? You *loco* or something?"

I twisted away from his uncle.

"I'll be there to see him race," Twig's uncle said, sneering at me. "I'll be there."

chapter twelve

"Darius, I know you mean well, but you're putting too much pressure on your friend," Mom said.

"He said he liked the pressure," I said.

"What's he going to say? His best friend is bringing his family to see him run in a race, and maybe change his young life, and it's up to him to do well. How old is he, anyway?"

"Sixteen," Brian piped up. "He just made it, too."

"Sixteen-year-olds shouldn't have that kind of pressure on them," Mom went on.

"I just want him to do well," I said.

"Boy, you are smart and you have a good heart, but you shouldn't put pressure on other people if you can't do anything to help them," Mom said. "I don't think that's right."

"You think I should tell him not to run?"

"You can't do that now," Mom said.

"So you're just putting pressure on me, and you can't do anything about it, right?"

"No, I can do something about you," Mom said. "I can teach you something that you need to know, and that's what I'm doing. You love your friends and you give them the benefit of the doubt, but you don't put them out there by themselves to do your work. And don't be getting into my face, boy."

"Yes, ma'am."

What did she know? She was so busy with her own problems, she couldn't see anything else. She didn't know what running meant to Twig, or what his succeeding meant to me. What she was doing was drifting into our problems for the moment, and then she would drift out again. The way she always does.

"Mom, how come Twig is Darius's best friend, and not me?" Brian asked.

"Because brothers are different than friends," Mom said.

"Why?" Brian asked.

"Because they are," Mom said.

"Why?"

"So his mother and grandmother are coming?" Mom took the last piece of toast, then offered it to me, and I shook my head.

"They want to see how he does," I said.

"Well, me and Brian will come down, too," Mom said. "Just to give him some support."

I didn't want Mom to watch Twig run, and I didn't want to tell her to stay away. I wanted to find my own way of handling things, tell her how I was going to do it, and just go about my business. Instead, I grabbed my notebook and told her I had to go to the library.

The Countee Cullen Library was fairly full for a week night. I found a copy of *Cane* by Jean Toomer and read it in a corner. It didn't make a lot of sense, but I liked the mix of prose and poetry. I liked even more the way it took me away from the thoughts buzzing around my head.

The Saturday sky was bright gray, threatening to rain. The track team arrived in the bus provided by the city, and I helped unload the equipment.

"Everybody, compete within yourselves," the coach was saying to the athletes as they gathered before him. "You know your times, you know your distances, and you know your bodies. If each of you achieves his best time, we have a good chance of winning this meet."

Warm-ups. Runners eyeing one another, some talking, trying to sound confident to an opponent who was trying just as hard. Judges going around checking rosters, asking questions about eligibility. With everything in place, I sat on the sideline, in front of Twig's family. Mom and Brian came over and nodded, then sat next to me.

I watched as Twig's uncle looked at Mom and then turned away. Asshole.

Twig's grandmother got up and sat next to Mom.

There were a handful of reporters and they were talking to one of the other coaches. Then they called a runner over. He was a tall kid, thin, loose. A photographer was shooting pictures of him as the other reporters interviewed him. All the way through the interview, he was moving, stretching, touching his toes. Pulling his feet up behind him.

"I can stretch as good as he can, anyway," Twig said when he came over to me. I was going to ask who *he* was when Coach Day came up. "That's Jameson," he said. "He's got a chance to break the meet record in the 3200. There are probably a dozen scouts in the stands watching him today."

"Scouts?" I asked.

"Guys who sell reports to colleges, or even some alumni who check on local athletes," Coach said.

"They sitting in the stands with stopwatches and stuff?" Twig asked. "See who does the fastest 100, the fastest 200, stuff like that?"

Coach looked at Twig. "Mostly longer races," he said. "If you can come anywhere near Jameson, they'll be writing your name down, too. You can bet on that."

I felt someone sit next to me and saw that it was Twig's uncle.

"When are you going to run?" he said to Twig. "I don't have all day."

"This is my uncle," Twig said.

"Oh, you've got a good little runner here." Coach Day extended his hand and Twig's uncle extended his. "Unfortunately, he's up against one of the best in the district today. All those reporters are here to see that kid in the maroon jumpsuit do his thing."

Twig's uncle looked over to where Jameson was still being interviewed. There was a woman with a small camera in front of him.

"How old is he?" Twig's uncle asked. Good question.

"Eighteen. A half dozen colleges are interested in him. They even called me to ask how good I think he is."

"How good is this boy?" The uncle points toward Twig.

"He's coming along," Coach said. "He's coming along. They're going to have the sprint prelims, and then they'll have the 3200 after that. Normally they'd have the 1600 first, but the press wants to get the 3200 in so they can write up their stories for tomorrow's paper and still have time to party tonight. Jameson is the story."

Coach went back to his position on the sideline. Twig's uncle returned to the stands and sat two rows up from Twig's mom. He was going to be aloof all the way. Twig sat next to me.

"How you feeling?" I asked.

"Nervous good," he said. "I'm edgy, like I want to be."

"The coach said if you just stay close to this guy, they'll notice you," I said. "You ever see him before?"

"Yeah, one time I was running around the reservoir and he was running at the same time," Twig

74

said. "He started first and I was just running after him, using him to pace myself. I liked the way he ran and I ran with him, not thinking about much because I was just exercising. Then he took off for a short distance, and then he stopped. It was like he was finishing a race. Later I saw his picture in the paper and then I knew who he was. I always wanted to run against him."

"You think you need to relax more?"

"No, I need to be nervous," Twig said. "It's a good feeling."

There weren't any surprises in the sprint semis. Black and Latino kids won; white kids who expected to lose made a showing and gave up.

In the infield, white kids threw the javelin farther, pole-vaulted higher, and shot-put farther. Black and Latino kids showed up, got eliminated, and put their sweats back on.

The high jump was mixed, with kids of all races doing fairly well.

Then came the 3200.

There were nine runners in the race. Jameson had the inside lane, and Twig was in the fifth. When the gun went off, the racers broke together, but one of the runners from the far outside cut quickly across the track and took the lead. He wore the same maroon-and-gold uniform as Jameson and was going to be the rabbit, the one to set the pace.

He sprinted ahead of the field quickly and then settled into a steady rhythm. For the first two laps, Twig was fourth, but by the third he had moved up behind the two runners from Ridgefield. He didn't look good. Several times he wiped at his face, and I wondered if something was bothering him.

Twig's uncle had moved above and behind me. I glanced back at him and saw him sitting with his hands folded on his lap, his head cocked to the side.

"The runners are on pace for a new district record!" came the announcement over the loudspeaker system. Several of the reporters looked at their wristwatches. I wondered what they could tell from that.

At the beginning of the fourth lap, the runners still held the same position except for some jockeying at the rear of the pack. Twig was still five yards behind Jameson, but there were fifteen yards between him and the fourth runner. My legs were moving with Twig's. I could feel them, but I couldn't stop them. I tried to imagine myself flying above the track, looking down at the lead runners, thinking about what I would want to do.

The runner who was the rabbit in the race moved up slightly as Jameson neared him. Did Jameson say something? Could he feel Twig's presence?

By the end of the fifth lap, the kid setting the pace had moved aside, letting Jameson pass him. Twig moved up quickly, but the rabbit picked up speed and Twig didn't make a move. Twig fell back a few feet, waited until they had passed the first turn, and then moved easily past the guy who had been setting the pace. They knew what they could do, what their roles were. But by the time they had finished the second turn, headed down the long stretch, Twig was another ten yards behind Jameson.

"Jameson is still on pace for a district record!"

Now it was no longer "the runners," it was Jameson. They were circling the 400-yard track in four to six seconds over a minute. A man standing with the reporters gave them the stats for each lap. And at the end of each lap, the loudspeaker announced that Jameson was still on pace.

There was a buzz from the crowd, a rising murmur that seemed to grow as the runners started the final quarter. A lapped runner moved and let the leaders past. Jameson looked strong, his long arms and legs moving effortlessly, efficiently, along the black cinder track. Twig moved to within a few yards of Jameson, and they were running almost as if they were a team.

As they went around the far turn of the eighth lap, Jameson took a quick peek over his shoulder. He saw Twig and turned toward the track. He seemed unconcerned. Off to my right, I saw one of the reporters stand up for a better view.

Nearing the final turn, they were two yards apart. Jameson glanced toward the finish line, and I thought he was calculating just how much energy he had to expend.

Then they were on the straightaway.

"It could be a district record!" blared over the loudspeaker.

Less than a hundred yards to go.

"It's going to be a race to the finish!"

I felt too weak to stand, almost too afraid to look.

Twig moved a step out and went past Jameson with sixty yards to go. Jameson seemed surprised, but his effort was huge as he pumped his arms furiously. He closed a step, but no farther.

Twig crossed the finish line mere inches ahead of Jameson. His hands shot into the air. He ran a few yards farther before stopping and bending over, his arms across his chest. Then he stood and turned to where he knew his family was, and where I was, and pumped his fists in the air.

Afterward, there were hugs all around. Guys from the school tried to lift Twig but let him slip to the ground, and he was lucky to catch himself. Reporters got to Jameson and to Twig. The announcer stated that it had to be verified, but that he thought Fernandez had just set a new district record.

A reporter walked over to Coach Day, who motioned for Twig's uncle to come from the stands.

I listened from a few feet away as Twig's uncle said something about people in his family having a lot of dedication. I tuned him out. Twig came to me, exhausted, and slapped my palms as I held them up.

"Was that sweet?" he asked. "Was that sweet?"

"It was sweet!" I said.

On the way back to the nabe Twig's uncle talked about character and, touching his own chest, how races are won by character and heart. He said that when he was young, he was the fastest boy on his block. But it was Twig's grandmother who spoke the most. Her face was lit up by an old-lady smile as she said again and again how excited she had been to see Twig run.

"You were such a small *niño*," she said. "No bigger than a handful. Look at you now. No, no, really, look at you!"

chapter thirteen

Does the hawk fly by thy wisdom?
  —Job 39:26

Saturday night and I was on Skype with Twig. I saw
he had a new poster on his wall and I asked him
about it.

"That's Saint Margaret of the Sacred Heart," Twig
said. "My aunt said I should put a saint up in my room
instead of worshipping football players."

"And you put her up?"

"No, my aunt did," Twig said. "And she's going to
stay up until my aunt goes back to the DR."

"You still floating from this afternoon?"

"No, man, I was thinking about it— Uh-oh, I gotta

go—I'm supposed to be doing the dishes. I'll call you later, okay?"

"No, wait, what were you thinking?" I asked.

"Like how easy it would have been for me not to have been running today," Twig said. "If my uncle Ernesto had got to my mom, I would have been pushing a broom around his store. It would have been so easy, Big D. That shit is scary. Look, I gotta go!"

"Later."

I hung up and flopped on my bed. Twig was right. It wouldn't have mattered how fast he was, or how much heart he had, if his uncle had killed it. It just wouldn't have mattered.

I took out the story I had sent to the *Delta Review*. It was a good story and they had got into it. But if they didn't publish it, then it wouldn't matter how good it was. Like Mr. Ramey had said, colleges were interested in what did happen, not what could have happened. The editors were asking me to make it clear whether the boy had faith in the dolphins to save him. I knew I needed to find the truth. What was it Miss Carroll had said? All of fiction is truthful. What you create is your own truth and no one can take that away or change it.

Did the boy, swimming farther and farther away

from the safety of the shore, think the dolphins would be there for him? Or was he just finding a way to give up?

And why had I given him a bad leg?

"What we need to do," said Reverend Allen as he stood at the podium at Thursday-night services, "is to show the world that no matter what the world says, there are people in this community who are *still right* with God! Can you *hear* me?"

"*Still* right!" came from the small gathering.

"Who are *still right* with God!" Reverend Allen repeated. "They may not be right with the electric company. They may not be right with the gas company. And they may not be right with their husband or wife, but they are still right with God! And when you're right with God, nothing else matters except for a little inconvenience.

"I remember an elderly sister I went to visit about this time last year. I found her sitting up in her kitchen in the dark because she hadn't been able to pay her light bill. I said, 'Sister, it's a shame you have to sit up here in the dark. Let me go out and buy you some candles.

"She reached over, put her hand on mine, and

said, 'Reverend Allen, it's just a small bother because my God can see in the dark!'"

"Amen!"

"We got people in this community who will always be right with God and some people who need a little help. That's why I want to get some church members to that party the mayor is throwing this Saturday night. All I want you to do is wear one of the armbands we wear for parades. We have enough of them. And just walk around and let yourself be seen by the young folks. Just let them see that God is making his presence known even at something as light as a little October celebration. We don't want the headlines to read that our community did worse than the community downtown, or that there was any trouble up here in Harlem. From what I hear, they had quite a few young men patrolling the streets during their party downtown to make sure that nothing went wrong. We're going to show up, and show out for God, and ask his holy blessing on our community and on the celebration. Can I get an amen?"

He got several amens and then the choir started singing.

Brian and I didn't usually go to Thursday-night services because it was a school night. I didn't mind going to church, I just didn't want to go all the time, especially at night. Mama had started going when the store cut her Thursday hours.

When services were over, Reverend Allen said, "Anyone who needs to talk, please tarry and pray, please stay." Mama said she was staying, but that me and Brian could go on home if we wanted.

"She said she keeps falling behind no matter what she does," Brian said. "I asked her what happened, and she said nothing happened, that she just keeps slipping back all the time. She said she might start looking for an extra job."

I knew she wouldn't, but I didn't want to say that to Brian. Mom wasn't making it and I knew she wasn't. Brian was beginning to see it, too, but I didn't want to spell it out for him. Not yet.

"We need to hit the lottery," my brother said.

"You got some money to play the lottery?"

"Okay, first we rob a bank." My little brother was letting his imagination loose again. "Then we lay low for two weeks, then take all the money we get from the bank and buy a kazillion scratch-off tickets. Then whatever we win with that, we buy two kazillion lotto tickets and hit the lotto and get rich."

"Suppose we get caught robbing the bank?" I asked.

"Then I say you made me do it and I go free while you go to jail forever," Brian said.

"Good plan," I said.

chapter fourteen

The happiness, and relief, I felt when Twig won the race stayed with me. Brian kidded me about it, and Mom, as she does, began to worry about it.

"You can't live somebody else's life," she said, frowning.

Okay, I knew that. I knew that Twig's winning wasn't mine to own, or to keep. But it *was* mine to hold up and say, "Hey, this is a win for all of us."

Brian came with us to Marcus Garvey Park for the party.

We watched people setting up vending stands, and soon smoke and scents from all over the Caribbean competed for air space. There were a few guys, old brown-as-coconut guys, playing chess at some of the concrete tables. Black heavy-chested women found spots on the benches, and the steel band— I was surprised it was all girls and women—set up their instruments on the grass.

The mayor showed. She pulled up in a limousine, dressed in jeans, a bright orange sweater, and heels that made her taller than the black guy I took to be her bodyguard. A sound crew set up a mike, and the mayor said she was glad to see so many people out.

"We've got a lovely, lovely day," she said. "A *New York* kind of day!"

There was some cheering, and she went to the first vendor she saw and bought a hot dog.

The steel band was good, and I wondered if they were from the neighborhood.

"They sound like professionals!" Twig said.

They played some corny music, make-believe calypso, which everybody seemed to like, and a few couples got up to dance.

"We should have brought some hot dogs and cooked them to sell to people," Brian said.

"You can't cook," I said.

"Why you always have to get so technical, man?"

We watched for a while without talking and then

Twig told us about a phone call he had received.

"Some racing official dude wants me to run in Delaware," he said. "I don't think I want to do that. I asked Coach Day about it and he said it was a bad idea, too."

"He just said it was bad?"

"He said they were trying to build up the Delaware games to rival the Penn relays. But if they bring in a lot of the top runners and I have a bad day and come in fourth or fifth, then it would just look like I couldn't compete against the top guys. But if I just did really well in the high school meets, and added that on to beating Jameson, I would get more attention from colleges."

"What do you think?"

"I don't know. I like to run, but I don't like to plan strategy and stuff about what I want to get out of it," he said. "Running should be, like, fun—like the way you look at it. You and me felt the same way when I ran. We were just glad I won. In a way we—I was hoping for somebody to come along and say, 'Hey, maybe we can get you into a college on a free ride.' But even if that doesn't happen, I still think I'd like to compete. What do you think?"

"I'll go down to Delaware with you," I said.

"Yeah, man!" Twig put his hand up, palm down, and I put mine out, palm up. He slapped my hand hard. "I knew you were going to say that! I want to run against the good dudes. I do!"

Twig was glad I had understood him. I was glad, too. I could look at him and see what he wanted. Twig wasn't down with college. He would have worked in his uncle's store if he could still train and run. For Twig the race was what it was all about, testing himself and seeing what he could do. That whole bit was so on the money. He didn't have to worry about what anybody else was doing, just himself. Maybe it wasn't ambitious enough for some people, but for Twig, it was life.

A yellow city school bus came and a group of kids—they looked about nine or ten, and all dressed down—got off. They lined up two by two and marched into the park.

"Yo, Brian, here come your peeps!" Twig said to my brother. "Only they got their wives with them."

"They look Latino," Brian said. "They must be *your* peeps."

"You can't be Latino until you're a teenager," Twig said.

"Twig, that is soooo stupid!" Brian said.

"I know." Twig smiled.

Some Parks Department people met with the kids and the women with them and spoke for a moment. Then there was a lot of nodding and the women had the kids stand in a circle while they were setting up another sound system.

Three white girls—they looked like high schoolers—were sitting on the grass near us, laughing and drinking sodas. I remembered what some people were saying about white people buying property in Harlem and taking over the community. The girls didn't seem like much of a threat.

I saw a few people from the church, wearing their armbands as Reverend Allen had asked them, just walking around smiling and saying hello to people.

"My uncle thinks I should buy new track shoes," Twig said. "He doesn't know anything about running, but he just needs to get his mouth into everything."

"Is he going to buy them?" Brian asked.

"He said he would," Twig answered. "But he can't tell the difference between a good pair of shoes and a wack pair. You need to find shoes you're comfortable in. If you got to run according to the way the shoe feels, then you got a problem. All he knows is

Air Jordans and he saw them on television."

"That's dumb," Brian volunteered.

"Yeah, but it's family, too."

"Let him buy you a pair like the ones you won the race with," Brian said.

"Yo, check this out!" Twig said. "I think the steel band is going to play for the kids."

The kids from the school buses, the boys in dark suits and the girls in dresses, gathered in front of the steel band.

"Ladies and gentlemen." The woman speaking was short, dark, and a little pudgy. "I would like to present to you the young dancers from La Vals de Brindis. Our sound system isn't working today, but the Jamaican Lasses will try to play for us. Thank you."

A black woman took the microphone and said that the Jamaican Lasses would not just *try* but that they would *play*.

"And our first number will be 'The Blue Danube Waltz,' by Johann Strauss."

The band started playing the waltz and the kids started dancing.

"Yo, man, they're great!" Twig said. "I've heard of

these kids. They do ballroom dancing and they're, like, eight years old."

They were frigging great. It was as if a group of very short classical dancers had suddenly appeared from another era. They danced as if no one were there except their partners, as if no one had the right to come between the young boys moving gracefully in a circle they held in their minds and the young girls trusting themselves to their arms.

The kids changed the nature of the party, turning it suddenly into something magical and beautiful.

Pop! Pop! Pop!

A scream!

Down! Down! Everybody down!

Oh my God! Oh my God! They're shooting.

A gray figure, hood half covering his face, running across the park. He turns, stumbles, lifts his arm.

Pop! Pop! Pop!

There are people running everywhere. Women are pushing children out of the way.

The sound of a police siren. A whistle. The kid dancers are crawling on their hands and knees back to their bus. A policeman stops them and boards the bus to check it out. He clears it and then motions the kids on.

A circle of black women, their arms outstretched, surrounds the children.

Then, silence.

Down the street there are guys in hoodies, their pants down around their asses, running.

People on the ground are beginning to get up.

The shoot-by is over.

So is the party in Marcus Garvey Park.

chapter fifteen

The falcon soars over the drabness of the city, hardly noticing the occasional bits of color in the streets below, the cars, the dark figures it knows are people. The falcon has no anger, no rage. Anger and rage demand knowing, demand looking into faces and feeling what another creature feels. No one does this in a war. In a war, one finds what one must destroy, and then one swoops down for the kill. There can't be pity, or weighing of arguments, and never understanding. No, never understanding.

I am the raptor, and you are the prey. I will swoop from the heavens and kill you. As you thrash about in agony, I will eat your flesh, and I will not hear your cries, the feeble beating of your wings against me, the quivering of your legs as I tear at your heart.

I am the raptor, and you are the prey.

"So, is she going to be okay?" Mom was carrying a dozen eggs in a plastic shopping bag.

"Yeah, the bullet hit her shoulder, but she's only two—not even two—and the doctors don't even think it'll leave a scar." Mr. Watson sat on the stoop, his coffee in a cup beside him. "I just wonder what kind of people got to bring a gun to a party."

"Well, God was looking out for her," Mom said, adjusting the package in her arms to carry upstairs. "That's a blessing."

"We need some civilizing!" Mr. Watson said. "We don't need no more blessing and no more scribbling on the walls about how we love another dead black child!"

"Brian home?" Mom to me, avoiding Mr. Watson's anger.

"Yeah."

"Supper's going to be ready in a half hour," she said.

I watched as Mom went into the house.

Sammy Hines from the barbershop came over and leaned against the banister. "Hey, Darius, how you doing, youngblood?"

"I'm good," I answered.

"Did you know that Watson here thinks these steps are going to get up and walk away if he don't sit on them?" Sammy asked. "That's why he's here every day."

Old friends talking old-friends talk. Sweet.

"I'm sorry if I get so mad," Mr. Watson said, "but you know how old this mess gets? Was a time an old dude like me could look at his life and think it wasn't so bad, because he had made a little bit of a path for some young folks. Didn't even make a difference if the young folks knew it or not—an old man could remember what he'd been through. You know what I mean?"

"Yeah, kind of," I said.

"Now we're burying our young people, so what we got to look back on?"

"I'm looking for some exercise to keep my body young in case I think of getting married again," Sammy said.

"Getting married again?" Mr. Watson shook his head slowly. "How long you been married to Hazel? Forty years? Damn near fifty years, and she's the only one who can stand you. What you going to marry next? It better be a bucket of Kentucky Fried Chicken because that's about the only thing you can handle.

And you better marry it on a day when you got your teeth in."

Old men talking. Finding good vibes in being old men. Sweet.

"Lord, this man is hard on me!" Sammy said, grinning. "He don't show me no mercy!"

"Look at these fools coming down the street with their pants hanging around their hips looking like four-year-olds," Mr. Watson said.

"You know they keep their pants low to get some air on their brains, don't you?" Sammy said.

I looked down the street and saw Midnight and Tall Boy coming our way. I saw Tall Boy point to me as they neared.

"Yo, Darius, where your girl?" he said. "She out running some races?"

"Twig ran his race last Saturday," I said. "Won it, too."

"Yeah, yeah." Midnight looked down the street. "How you doing, Mr. Watson?"

"Doing good," Mr. Watson said. "Ain't seen you in church for a while. See your mother there every Sunday."

"You know how that goes." Midnight hunched his

shoulders. "What y'all think about that shooting at the party? That was some foul mess."

"Pretty little girl," Sammy said. "All eyes. I think she's a little Muslim girl. But what kind of fool brings a gun to a party? Maybe they think shooting people is a lot of fun."

"Yeah, we got some names," Tall Boy said. "And we got the answer to the question they throwing."

"You got the names of the people who did the shooting?" Mr. Watson looked up. "You call the police? You know you don't have to give them your name. Just tell them who did the shooting."

"That ain't the way it works in the street," Midnight said. "What they throwing is 'Are we some kind of punks going to let people just shoot our little sisters and shit?' They want to know what kind of heart we got. The police don't have nothing to do with it. This is a heart thing. We got enough heart and they'll keep their stuff on their own blocks, you hearing me?"

"What I'm hearing is you saying that they came into your area and laid down some stink, and now you want to lay down some more stink to prove you can outstink them," Mr. Watson said. "Why you think that's a good idea?"

"You don't know what's happening, old man," Midnight said, shaking his head. "The set just blew by you, and you didn't even see it coming. You like Peter Pan over here. Him and his little fairy friend going to run around in shorts and take over the world."

"At least Twig is doing something with his life," I said, feeling stupid as the words came out. "There were a lot of college scouts at that meet."

"Guess what." Midnight pushed himself up in front of me. "I don't give a fuck! How's that? I don't give a fuck!"

Tall Boy started off first, with his hand, palm up, behind him as he bopped down the street. Midnight ran behind him and slapped him five as they both laughed.

"He don't give a *what*?" Mr. Watson turned to Sammy. "What's that supposed to mean?"

"What he thinks is that there's some power in what he just said," Sammy said. "He thinks that if he gets up in your face and says he don't care about nothing, you're supposed to step back and let your jaw drop or something. What he don't realize is that he's going to reach a point where nobody cares about him, either."

"I'll tell you when he's going to find out that nobody gives a fuck," Mr. Watson said. "When he's sitting up in a jail with a whole bunch of knuckleheads just like him with nowhere to go except to lunch for some boiled frankfurters and mashed potatoes. When he's done that for about three years in a row, he's going to start getting a clue."

"No, he won't," Sammy said. "People like him don't never get a clue. They go through all their lives talking to themselves and telling themselves how wonderful they are. Then they look around and start complaining about life ain't fair."

"I guess you just have to avoid guys like that," I said.

"Can't avoid them." Mr. Watson shook his head and looked down the street as if he were looking off into the past. "You used to be able to avoid them, walk on the other side of the street, look the other way when they passed by, go to a different pool hall or barbershop. Now it's hard. Look at that little girl. She didn't go to that party looking to hurt nobody. She sure wasn't looking for the fool that shot her."

"Good thing she wasn't hurt bad," Sammy said. "Soon as I heard what happened, I felt bad. You see her picture in the paper? Nothing but eyes on that baby. Nothing but eyes!"

"Yeah, I heard they got guns hidden away up on the roofs," Mr. Watson said. "So sooner or later that young fool is going to kill somebody. Sooner or later."

"Well, thank God that little girl wasn't hurt worse or killed. They said she'll get over it pretty soon," Sammy said. "But you know the newspapers are going to run it. Child shot in Harlem! They're going to keep it alive until they run out of damn ink."

I said good-bye to Sammy and Mr. Watson and started upstairs.

"Thank God that little girl wasn't hurt worse or killed," Sammy had said, meaning the words. But how could he tell how badly she was hurt? How badly is a two-year-old hurt when she's watching other children dance and suddenly a pain rips through her body? How could anyone tell how badly she was hurt?

chapter sixteen

The falcon soars high above the streets, looking down at the figures below, looking for what he will eat. The idea of mercy is lost. The creatures below, the ones who don't give a fuck, have no mercy to give. But that is all right for the falcon. He is not looking for friends.

Twig called to tell me that the little girl who was shot was out of the hospital. I told him what Midnight and Tall Boy had said, about getting revenge, which Twig thought was stupid. Which everybody with half a brain *knew* was stupid.

"So how's your story going?" Twig asked. "You finished it yet?"

"Just about," I lied.

Miss Carroll had said that you didn't have to tell everything in a piece of fiction, but you had to *know* everything. I didn't think she was right. I thought there were feelings and mysteries in stories that the author might have to think about even after a story had been published. What I knew was that I was worried about the story. It hadn't meant that much to me as I wrote it. It had been just another story, but then I had sent it off, and the letter saying they might publish it made it more important. Showing the letter to Miss Carroll made me feel good, and what she had said about it, that being published would change who I was, came as a surprise.

"You're still the same person, of course," she had said. "But for many reasons people tend to look at you differently. Sometimes at parties you can hear people being introduced as So-and-so who was published in *The New Yorker* or some other magazine."

I wanted that kind of party. Where people had value because of something they had created, or painted, or performed. It sounded like a get-together of my kind of people.

The story. A boy, who lives in an orphanage, is depressed. He wonders what his future is going to be. The beach is good for him, especially on colder days, when it is nearly deserted. Then one day he starts to swim out toward an island that is a bit far. How far is it? As he swims, he realizes that he is in an area almost too far for him to return. He starts back but grows tired. Then, from somewhere, a dolphin appears and nudges him toward shore.

He is drawn to the cold waters and to the distant island. He pushes himself to swim a little farther, despite his bad leg. Why does he have a bad leg? Does that just make him less capable than the other children at the orphanage? Does he think he is less capable? When he is not in the water, does he think of the dolphins? Or does he just wonder if they will be there to save him if he swims too far? Does the reader have to know?

The editor wants the story to be clearer. He wants to know if it is a story of hope and faith or a story of despair. Sometimes, in my mind, the two are so close together. So close.

chapter seventeen

In Riverside Park with Twig. He was stretching. With one leg on the top of the fence he brought his forehead to his knee and held it there for several seconds. Then the other leg was up and he was stretching his other hamstring.

"So Coach Day brings this guy up to me. Mr. Day introduces the guy as Eddie and says he's an old friend," Twig said. "Then this guy starts asking me what size shoes I wear, and what kind of sweats do I like and stuff like that, and right away, I'm not feeling good about him."

"His name is just Eddie? No last name?"

"Right." Twig brought his leg down, put his hands on his hips, and started rotating his upper body.

"I asked him his last name and he's saying this and saying that, but not giving me his name. I kept pushing it and he's like, 'Oh, you're so suspicious.' Then he tells me he's a consultant for athletic programs. But he's, like, keeping a distance. You know what I mean?"

"No."

"He's talking, but he's not saying anything," Twig said.

"Yeah, like he doesn't want to commit himself," I said.

"Yeah. He's not creepy, but he's mysterious and stuff," Twig said. "I don't like mysterious. I like straightforward. That's what I like about you. You got nothing mysterious going on."

"What are you talking about, Twig? I've got lots of mystery going on," I said. "You think you know everything about me?"

"Yep." Big smile on a face that lights up when he's happy. Twig is open, too, and he's right, that is where we connect. "I'm thinking that maybe I don't want to go to Delaware. If it's going to mean hooking up with people I don't trust. I kind of knew where this guy was coming from. . . . He thinks I can run, Coach told him that, I guess, and he can do something with it. But . . ."

"Hey, Twig?"

"What?"

"You know, when you were running against that guy, that Jameson, and you said you were feeling the pain, and you had to fight through it?"

"Yeah?"

"Maybe meeting guys like this is part of the pain of moving on," I said. "You know, you and me hang together tough, and we like each other, but all I'm doing is hoping for you and cheering you on. Maybe the pain you have to get through is all the bullshit connected with running. Like Jameson had that rabbit pacing him, and that was bullshit because he didn't need that guy. And the guy who was the rabbit was just out there being a rabbit. That's really bullshit."

"I bet you he dreams about taking off one day," Twig said. "Instead of just being a rabbit setting a pace, he'll take off and set a record or something."

"Yeah, but it's just a dream because he's got himself trained to be a rabbit," I said.

"I know what you mean," Twig said. "I know it. Look, I'm going to run for fifteen minutes with the weights, just to get loose."

"If it feels even a little bad, even a little, stop right away," I said. "I don't like the idea that much, anyway."

Twig had read in a book where a marathon runner ran with a five-pound weight around his waist, and he was going to try running with a three-pound weight to build up his strength.

We coordinated our watches and then Twig took off with an easy pace. From where I sat, it didn't look as if he was even noticing the weight, but I thought I'd be able to tell when he came back. If he stiffened up, then it was a bad idea.

I don't know how we got to calling the field Twig was running on Greeney's, but that's how we had known it for years. I watched as my friend ran. Twig had found a real joy in running, had found a pleasure and a freedom that he didn't have anywhere else in his life. It was something he could do, a statement that his body could make to the world. I watched him run, looking free and happy. Holding on to the feelings that running brought to him, being alive with those feelings, and cherishing them. The guy who wanted to scout for athletic programs wanted Twig to be something else. He wanted a runner who would put aside his own feelings to be useful to someone—or something—else. I had a bad feeling about that guy.

Maybe that was what Twig needed to do, to fight through the pain of being in the big sports world. It was something I envied about Twig. There was a competition, a "my strength against your strength" kind of thing that he had going on. Jameson and Twig were runners and they had run head to head. That was good. That was the way it should be, I thought. But if you were smart, it never happened that way. Midnight wasn't going to come up to me and challenge me to an IQ test. No way—he would just come up and punch me in the face. And if that didn't work, maybe he would cut me, or shoot me.

I remembered a book I had read—*The Gay Genius*—about a Chinese poet named Su Tungpo. He had taken tests to be a civil servant as well as a poet and had been successful. That was what I wanted. I would face down Tall Boy in a poetry slam and leave him bleeding and whimpering in front of a dead mike. *A todas cool!*

Twig jogged back and said it felt good. "I noticed at the end that I was feeling it a little," he said. "I don't know how fat people carry the extra weight around."

"You going to keep carrying the weights when you run?" I asked.

"What do you think?"

"It could mess up your rhythm," I said. "Why not just carry them around when you're not running? That should build you up, too."

Twig gave me a look, then sat down next to me. "That's really a smart idea," he said. "Coach never comes up with anything like that. You know, I think you've got two brains. One sits on top of the other one."

"Twig, that's so stupid, man."

"Yeah," he said, looking out over the park, "I know."

chapter eighteen

"So we have three different kinds of birds here." The tall, thin speaker was all angles and nervousness as she spoke. Her English accent seemed just perfect in the light rain. "Each bird has certain advantages for the handler, but it must be remembered that, essentially, they are wild creatures that cooperate with humans only because they see us as hunting partners. These are not 'friendly' birds by any stretch of the imagination."

"Do you actually hunt with a hawk?" an older man asked.

"I've been hunting with hawks and falcons for over twenty years," the woman answered. "My grandfather had quite a reputation as a hunter and trainer of birds."

"How much do they cost?" Twig asked. It was Saturday morning, and me and Twig were at the Brooklyn Botanic Garden to hear the lecture about hunting birds.

"To buy a sound bird in England could cost anywhere from fifty to four hundred pounds, depending on where you made your purchase," the woman answered. "But the real costs come later in the upkeep and care of the bird. A bird that is poorly handled is most often a bird that will simply fly away or, even more likely, die."

"How about the equipment?" Twig asked. "Is that expensive?"

"Are you thinking of buying a bird?" the woman asked. "Because if you are, I would very much advise against it. New York has several wild falcons that do very nicely on their own, but it would be a mistake to think that a person of your age would have the time, the incredible amount of patience, or the facilities to care for a bird for even a week."

Another man asked if falcons had ever been used in war, and the woman said she didn't believe so. "There was some talk about the Germans using them in France to intercept messages sent by pigeons," she said. "I haven't read anything that verifies that. And might I add, I'm always disappointed when someone asks me about using these birds in war or to fight. The relationship with a raptor is one of cooperation between the bird and its handler, and best achieved when the handler respects the bird."

We were shown all the equipment that hunters used with the birds—the hoods to cover their eyes and keep them calm, the different kinds of gloves people wore to protect their hands and wrists from the talons, and even the kinds of cord used when the birds were first training.

The lecture lasted an hour and a half and stretched into two with all of the questions people were asking. When it was over and Twig and I were watching the lady put her birds back into their cages, I asked her if she thought people would start raising birds in the United States.

"There are clubs in Colorado, California, and other states," she said. "On the East Coast and in the Northwest. And of course, there are clubs all over South America. But I don't like to see birds abused."

"Why do you think we would abuse them?" I asked.

"Americans have the money to buy what they want"

was the quick answer. "But often not the patience to learn what to do with it. I do hope you don't consider buying birds here in Brooklyn."

No matter what she said, I was thinking about it. Looking at the falcon, so different from how I could ever be on the outside, but seeming so wise, so fierce in its gaze, thrilled me. It was how I wanted to be. Sure. Detached. Knowing I was master of everything I saw beneath me.

chapter nineteen

"You guys want spaghetti tonight?" Mom asked.

I tried to be enthusiastic about the spaghetti, but I know I didn't come off too well, because Mom touched my knee the way she did sometimes when she wanted to let me know she understood how I felt.

When we got to the house, we saw Twig sitting on the stoop. He was playing checkers against Sammy from the barbershop.

"Yo, what's going on?" I asked.

"Your boy here is teaching me how to play checkers," Sammy said. "So far he's got me learning how to win gracefully."

"I think he's cheating," Twig said. Broad smile, open. "I'm trying to explain to him that he's only supposed to think one move ahead, but he's sneaking in some extra thinking. I can tell because his ears are wiggling."

"Twig, that is so stupid."

"Yeah, I know," Twig answered.

"How come trouble always comes in bunches?" Sammy asked. He was looking down the street.

It was a group of guys, taking over the sidewalk as they came our way.

"Ignore them if they say anything to us," Sammy said. "They out looking for trouble and I'm not in a mood to volunteer."

There were five of them. I recognized Midnight and Tall Boy and I thought one of the others was Diablo Thompson, a stocky kid who was always in jail.

Sammy was a full-grown man, and nobody wanted to mess with him too tough. He had worked in the barbershop on Frederick Douglass Boulevard for years and had finally bought it. But he was right. There wasn't any use in looking for trouble, and we all looked at the checkerboard as Midnight and his friends got near us.

"Hey, ain't you the dude that runs?" Diablo spotted Twig.

"Yeah."

"Congratulations, and all that shit," Diablo said. "I saw your picture in the paper. They said you could fly!"

"He ain't that fast," Midnight said, stepping closer to Twig.

"He can beat your ass," Diablo said. "I've never seen your picture in no paper. No, no, yeah I did. Didn't they get you once for stealing newspapers, but then they noticed you couldn't read and had to let you go?"

Laughter. Midnight tensed up, but he didn't want to mess with Diablo.

"I can run faster than this faggot right now," Midnight said. "And I don't need to be in no newspaper to prove it."

"Let's see y'all race from the corner we just come from to this stoop," one of the other guys said. "First one gets here is the winner and the last one is the chump."

"Yeah, we can watch Midnight get his butt kicked." Diablo clapped his hands together. "Jerry, start them off!"

Twig shrugged.

He started walking with Midnight down to the

corner. It had to be nearly sixty yards, maybe even seventy. Midnight was walking close to Twig and I knew he was talking to him, trying to intimidate him. Twig got to the corner and turned around.

At first Midnight got down into a sprint starting position, then straightened up when he saw that Twig was standing up.

Mrs. Odums and Mrs. Liburd crossed the street and stopped to see what was going on.

"They're going to race," Diablo said. "First one gets here is the winner."

"Oh, the boys always used to run in Jamaica," Mrs. Liburd said. "Anytime you saw two or more boys, they had to rip and run up the road to see who was the faster."

"Boys like to run," Mrs. Odums said. For some reason she liked that and nodded her head in approval.

Down the street, the boy Diablo had called Jerry lifted his hand up, and I could see he was saying something, but I couldn't hear it. Then he brought his hand down and Midnight took off. Twig started second but caught up to Midnight within a few yards. They ran halfway and Midnight was beginning to fade. At the end of the race, it was Twig reaching us first and Midnight standing fifteen yards away, bent over, hands on his knees, trying to catch his breath.

"Dude ate you up and he didn't even break a sweat!" Diablo said. "You couldn't've caught him if you were on the A train. Slow-assed punk! You need to go home and borrow your mama's sneakers!"

Laughter.

"He's so fast!" Mrs. Odums pointed at Twig. "He needs to be on a racing team. Do they have racing teams?"

Midnight came over to Twig and put out his left hand. When Twig went to take it, Midnight swung and hit him in the face.

I jumped up and Tall Boy stepped quickly in front of me and tried to punch me. I ducked down and he grabbed the back of my head and tried to push me down. He brought one leg up, and I felt it on my back. I grabbed his other leg and used my legs to lift him off the ground.

He grunted as he tried to grab me for balance. Straight up, I felt him falling and let myself fall on him.

Whoosh! He released his grip on me as the air came out of him.

Scrambling to my feet, I looked for Twig and saw him against the stoop post, dodging blows from

Midnight. I dropped my shoulder and ran into Midnight's side.

Someone came on my left side, and I turned to see Mrs. Odums trying to get between me and Midnight. Midnight reached across me and punched her face.

That was when Sammy got into it. He got to Midnight, put his arms around his waist, and threw him away.

"Whoa! Whoa! Break it up! Break it up!" This from Diablo. "We don't be fighting old people, man!"

Just as quickly as it started, it was over. Tall Boy was still trying to get up, Midnight was breathing hard, and Diablo and his other boys were taking charge of the sidewalk. Sammy looked Midnight up and down as if he wanted to start the fight again. Then he went and put his arms around Mrs. Odums.

"You okay?" he asked.

"They shouldn't fight," she said. "What happened to the running?"

"What y'all hitting an old woman for?" Jerry was up in Midnight's face. Midnight shook his head as he took a step back.

"Hey, Tall Boy, here's something for you, too," Diablo said.

Tall Boy looked up just in time to see Diablo's foot

swinging toward his face. He got his hands up late, and his head jerked back.

Bullies beating up bullies.

Diablo snapped his fingers, and he and the two others started walking away down the street. Midnight looked over at Sammy, then skulked off. Tall Boy was last. He got up holding his face and limped as he went after Midnight.

Somebody must have called Mom. She came out wearing an apron and carrying a little hammer she used to flatten meat. I went to her and put my arms around her.

There was a smear of blood across Twig's cheek and we took him upstairs. Mrs. Odums came with us. Twig's shoulders were shaking as the little dark woman wiped his face with the cold cloth Mom had given her.

"You going to be okay, honey," she said. "You're going to be just fine."

Mom made Twig drink some orange juice. I don't know how that was supposed to help, but it seemed to. Mom asked him to stay for dinner, and he said he had to go home.

"I'll go with him," I said.

Mom put her hand on my arm. "Darius . . . ?"

"I'll be okay," I said. "I'll be okay."

We went out into the hall, and I asked Twig if he wanted to talk. "We could go up on the roof," I said.

Twig said he wanted to go home.

The day had been hot, but it was cooling off a bit. I walked Twig to his house and tried to talk to him a few times, but he didn't answer. I had never seen him so down. But I understood.

I said good-bye at his front door, then turned and walked slowly back to my house. When I got to the house, Sammy was sitting on the stoop again.

"You all right?" he asked me.

"Yeah, I'm sorry about what happened."

"Wasn't your fault," Sammy said. "Some people just can't live a decent life. They got their heads messed up, and instead of changing their heads, they want to turn the world around so what's going on in their heads looks right to them. You can't mess with thinking like that. But you guys held your own. You did all right."

"Thanks."

I knew Mom would be full of good advice and I didn't want to hear any of it. Sammy was right. It didn't matter how you wanted to live if somebody else, somebody like Midnight or Tall Boy, or Diablo, wanted to mess it up. And I was thinking that Twig might have been right, too. Maybe they wouldn't let him run. Maybe they didn't want anyone to get out of the little crappy sewer lives they were in. If they harassed him enough, and filled his mind with enough negative crap, he would give it up. And I would give up trying to be a writer, or trying to do well in school, and just spend my life either running away, looking for a different place to live, or pretending I was dumb so I wouldn't stand out. It was a shitty way to live.

I went past my floor and up onto the roof. The smells from suppers being made in the apartments below drifted by, and a radio tuned to a Caribbean station sent up an old ska tune I used to like. A slight breeze lifted bits of paper from the gray asphalt matting that covered the roof. Two pigeons walked around the paper, and one jumped as the breeze swept the paper suddenly toward it.

The problem was that I didn't have any answers. I could come up with something for me to do, or Twig, but it wouldn't mean anything if I couldn't stop people from just punching the crap out of us. Sammy had said we had done all right. But he hadn't seen what was going on clearly enough. He saw that Twig could make Midnight miss him most of the time, and that I had got Tall Boy down on the ground. But what was going on inside us hadn't been nearly as good.

Twig had beaten Midnight, had done well, as anybody would have known he would, and that was why Midnight had hit him. Because he was good at something. And Tall Boy had jumped on me only because he thought I would be easy and he could get away with it. I hadn't done anything to him, hadn't even spoken to him.

And then Diablo had kicked Tall Boy for the same reason. He thought he could get away with it. There wouldn't be any price to pay that he would have to deal with. Tall Boy was on the ground, and even if he had gotten up, he wouldn't have fought Diablo.

Then I started thinking about my story again. Maybe the boy did have faith in the dolphins. Maybe he had just lost faith in everything else.

chapter twenty

I liked being on the roof as night fell.

Don't go dark on me, Darius.

It was as if I were invisible, and alone in my invisibleness. Looking down at the street, not being seen by the kids or the old-timers taking their places for the night, I felt untouchable. The way I felt Fury would be untouchable.

Day sounds, buses honking, children screaming, slowly gave way to the night sounds of blaring radios. The voices rising from the darkness became harsher, more strident. Words meant as curses and arrows lifted quickly. Across the street, the blue neon lights of Victory Tabernacle, House of Prayer, came on. I could see the abstractions, the angles and colors of a poet's eye.

Did you know that kestrels can see ultraviolet light? And that a peregrine falcon can see three times better than a human?

Twig pushed into my mind again. I imagined him running with a weight around his waist. Three pounds, then four, then five. I wondered if it would help his racing.

A light caught my eye. On a building across the street, over the Pioneer food market, there were shadowed figures. The night was warm and I thought they might have been crackheads paying the five dollars to sleep on someone's roof for the night. From where I sat, I could see four, perhaps five people. They weren't much more than shadows, and I moved against a chimney, into my own dark space. There was another, smaller glow, which I thought was probably a flashlight. Then I heard a shot.

It is Harlem. It is night. No big deal.

I looked over at the figures on the roof across the avenue. Had someone been murdered? Nobody was running. The bodies still seemed posed in casual attitudes. Then I remembered it was where Mr. Watson had said someone kept guns. They looked as if they were passing something around.

I watched them.

Movement on the roof. Silhouettes drinking from paper bags. Shadows smoking. One of them, it could have been Diablo, began to take something from the brick chimney. At first I couldn't see what it was, but then I saw a shiny object. They were hiding the guns behind loose bricks on the roof. That was why no one had found them.

More weight.

"You don't look good," I said. "You look like you've been up all night. What's up, Twig?"

"I decided to run in Delaware," Twig said. "Coach called me this morning and asked me. He called me at freaking seven a.m."

"Why are you upset?"

"You know what I feel?" Twig sounded shaky. "I feel like it's over for me. I'm going to go down to Delaware and run one last time and then forget about it. Coach was running his mouth about how this was going to be some bitching opportunity. How I could be a standout. I don't want to be a standout kind of guy. You know what I mean? If I'm standing out, then my family has to worry about some guy starting a fight with me or cutting me."

"What are you talking about?" I asked him. "This isn't about gangbanging, Twig."

"Yo, Darius, you're talking some good stuff, but at the same time you got me confused, man," Twig said. "You're always laying it out that the reason we're pushed around—that we're picked on—is that we stand out. You stand out a lot because you're friggin' smart, and I'm standing out because I can run. So you want to push standing out, and yet you don't want to be out. You getting what I mean?"

"If the world was different—"

"It ain't," Twig said quickly. "It's just the way you always run it. If we stand out, it's cool. But we got to pay a price for standing out and we don't have any guarantees we're going to get over."

"You get a scholarship, you can go away to college," I reminded him. "Get away from the streets and find your own world. Maybe even *make* your own world."

"No, not get away, Darius," Twig said. "You mean run away. We're talking about leaving our families here and looking for a new life. Maybe get rich and shit and marry white girls like the Yankees do. You want that?"

"The girls?"

"Okay, I can deal with the girls." Twig smiled. "But you want to be away from your people?"

"I don't know," I said. It was a question I hadn't wanted to deal with but one that was eating at me something fierce.

"Darius?" Twig, waiting for an answer.

"Twig, I think I do want to be away from here," I said. "Maybe I can come back and help, or something. I don't know. When I think about living a good life—you know, daydreaming and stuff—it's never about being around here."

"Amen to that, bro, but I don't want to be no Jesus or nothing like that," Twig said. "I just want to be me, man. I'm thinking I go down to Delaware just for me, to see what I can do. Then I walk away from everything. And you know something? You know what I know?"

"What?"

"I know if I walk away, then they'll forget me so fast it'll be like I never was," Twig said. "If I can't help them get over, then they don't need me."

"And Midnight and Tall Boy can say that they knew you weren't all that good in the first place," I added. "You want that?"

"What's gonna be is what's gonna be," Twig said

softly. "But I don't care anymore. It's all getting too hard."

"When you going to Delaware?"

"Thursday night," Twig said. "Coach Day said he can get you out of school and pay your way down, too. You coming with me?"

"He's going to pay my way, too?" I asked. "Why?"

"I think somebody else is footing the bill," Twig said. "Somebody—maybe that college scout—thinks we got something he can sell."

"That's what's scaring you?"

"I don't know what's scaring my ass," Twig said. "But I know I'm scared. What you think?"

"It could be something good," I said. "We should probably check it out."

"You going with me?" Twig asked. "If I'm going to run as hard as I can, I'm going to need somebody in my corner."

"Your folks can't go?"

"I need somebody who knows what I'm feeling," Twig said. "I need to look up in the sky and see Fury."

"We'll be there," I said.

chapter twenty-one

The trip down to Delaware took about two hours from Penn Station on 34th Street. It was me; Twig; Willie DeWitt, a sprinter and a running back; Willie's mom, who was pretty hot; Coach Day; and a short, kind of weird guy named Herb. Coach Day said that Herb was "connected" with a number of colleges.

"Willie, what you need to do is hit 10:02 just one time in the trials, or in the finals," Herb was saying. The Amtrak train had already pulled out of the station and was going to Newark, New Jersey. "So what the colleges can see is that you've got the moves for a halfback, but you also have the breakaway speed they're looking for."

"You think I can get a scholarship as a sprinter?" Willie asked.

"Too hard, too many guys fighting over less than five tenths of a second," Herb said. "I'm not saying it's not possible, but every day you have some kid coming up with a 10:01, a 10 flat, or a 9.9. But as a running back, especially someone with your size, you got a lot of potential."

"Willie can run," his mom said confidently. "Even when he was little, he could run fast."

"And Fernandez, what I want from you is even simpler. . . ." Herb leaned back in his seat.

"What *you* want from me?" Twig looked toward Coach Day.

"Let me put it this way," Herb said. "What would be best for you is for you to make the finals in either the 1500 or the 3000 and hit a fourth. That doesn't sound like a lot, but that puts you on record. When all the coaches across the country read the results, they're looking for young talent. Everybody knows everybody in these races. There aren't any secrets anymore.

"But half the guys running tomorrow are either college guys who don't have a consistency record, or they're past college and still hanging on to a dream. Either way, nobody is looking for them. What they're looking for is young guys. Guys like you and Willie. You show up fourth in the finals of either race, and they're going to see a high school kid they can reach out and grab."

"How come you want him to run?" I asked Herb.

"Because it's a chance for him to get a scholarship!" Coach Day said. "That's not rocket science, Austin."

"That's not what he's asking," Herb said. He took out a cigar and put it in his mouth.

"I don't think you can smoke on the train," Willie said.

"I'm not smoking it, just holding it in my mouth," Herb said. "What my man here is saying is, what's in it for me? That's right, isn't it?"

"Something like that," I said.

"He's working for Fernandez!" Coach Day came in again, this time sounding irritated.

"No, I'm working for both these kids, but I'm also building up my reputation as a person who can spot young talent. If Willie comes through, the football coaches are going to say, 'Oh, yeah, this is the young stud that Herb told us about. He was right.' And when they want somebody to fly to California or Red Neck, Georgia, or Perugia, Italy, they're going to call me and ask me to go for them and scout the kid they've heard about because they'll trust my judgment.

"And if Fernandez comes through, they'll call me up and ask me if he's really as good as that and I'll say—'Hey, he was running against the best young guys in the country and he did okay.' What more do they want? And they got to respect my judgment."

"You get paid?" Willie's mom asked.

"I'm glad I'm riding with some savvy people," Herb said.

chapter twenty-two

We got to Delaware and took a cab to the Holiday Inn. Me and Twig were in one room; Herb and Coach Day were in another room; Willie and a kid from Harrisburg, Pennsylvania, who was already there were in another room. Willie's mom had her own room. Herb gave us each twenty dollars to eat with.

"You can eat out or bring food back to your room," he said. "But don't order nothing from room service."

We checked out the room, and it was cool. There was a cabinet that had sodas and liquor, but that was locked. We turned on the television and ran through the channels until we found one we liked.

"Maybe this won't be so bad," Twig said.

I told myself three times not to ask Twig how he thought he was going to do in the morning.

Then I asked him.

"Herb told me I had to try harder in the 3000 than in the 1500, which sucks. He said I could run trials for the 1500, but he thinks I have a better chance in the 3000 open because the field is light. Sixteen guys running on a 400-meter track. That's not bad."

"And?"

"He still wants me to finish fourth," Twig said. "Don't take any chances. Just make sure I know where I am so I can work fourth place. The first four guys are listed in the reports they send to colleges. He thinks he can work a deal if I make fourth."

"You going to go for more?" I asked. "I don't see a risk."

"If I go for too much, I could get tired and fade bad at the end," Twig said. "I have to see how the race feels and what the pace is. What do you think?"

"If you come in fourth, then people like Herb take out their watches and notebooks to decide just how good you are, right?"

"Yeah."

"You want that?"

"My head is in a fight with my heart, man," Twig said. "My head is talking about being cool and doing what the man says. My heart is saying, 'Bust a move!' What you think I should do?"

"Could something else happen?" I asked. "Like, if you're cruising in fourth and some guy makes a move on you? Or, like, if everybody has somebody like Herb telling them to hang back for fourth?"

"And the guys out front are kicking it for one-two-three and the rest of them need to jump bad at the end for fourth?"

"Yeah, you could find yourself sweating for fourth."

"You know what else I was thinking? Maybe it's not even about me, man. Maybe all he wants to do is to show off Willie," Twig said. "And he's dancing around Coach by bringing me along."

"Let's go get Willie and find something to eat," I said.

We called Willie's room, but there was no answer. Then Twig and I went downstairs, found a 7-Eleven, and bought fruit and cookies and stuff to eat. We went back to the hotel and saw Willie in the lobby with the other guy.

"What's going on?" Willie asked.

"Just copped some fruit," I said.

"What do you run?" Twig asked the other guy.

"Sean," the guy answered. "Hurdles."

"Oh." Twig looked away as he nodded. "You play football, too?"

"Linebacker," Sean said.

Willie and Sean were on the fifth floor and me and Twig got off on the third. I asked Twig what he thought about Willie.

"I could smell the shit on him," he said.

"Yeah, me too," I said. "I don't know how he can run if he spends the night smoking weed."

"It's only a hundred yards," Twig answered. "You can do that on two breaths. Bam! Bam! Maybe even one breath. But I don't think he's serious enough to win anything. You don't go out looking for weed the night before you compete. And check this, his mom is sitting downstairs in the bar with Herb."

"Whatever."

chapter twenty-three

Morning. Coach Day was rubbing the tops of Willie's shoulders, and Herb was standing in front of him telling him what a great opportunity this was.

"You hit 10:02 and we can go to all the coaches in the country and lay it down the way they want to hear it," he said. "The only thing you got going against you is that your school didn't play in a tough football league."

"The games seemed tough to me," Willie said.

"They got a list of all the school districts in the country," Herb said. "Anything from the Deep South is going to be ahead of New York and New Jersey. Believe me. They figure they got two kinds of black dudes. One from the North and one from football country. Figure it out for yourselves."

Me and Twig had to leave the field for the start of the dash semis. We called to Willie to show them something.

The first two starts were false, with one kid, a short, wild-eyed dude, getting disqualified.

The next start was good and Willie came in second. Herb looked at his stopwatch and shook his head.

"10:03," he announced. "Got to pick 'em up and put 'em down, Willie."

While Willie was resting, Coach went over and talked to him. I didn't see how that was going to make him run any faster.

The first six guys from Willie's heat and the first five from the second heat ran in the boys' final. Willie was second again, but he hit 10:01 and Herb was jumping up and down. Willie had this huge grin on his face when he put on his sweat suit and jacket.

"I want you to do the same thing Willie did," Willie's mom said to Twig. Her face was all big smiles and gooey warm. "Just get on the track and run your little heart out!"

"Yes, ma'am," Twig answered.

Me, Twig, and Coach Day had to catch one of the shuttle buses to go over to where the distance races were being held. Willie, his mom, and Herb started back toward the hotel.

"How come Herb isn't going with us to see Twig run?" I asked Coach.

"Distance running is glory," Coach said. "Football is money."

When we got to the track, Coach went over to the officials and talked to them. They checked a roster and I saw Coach nodding.

"How you feeling?" I asked Twig.

"Butterflies," Twig said. "Good stuff."

Coach came back and told Twig that he was only entered in the 3000, not the 1500. "Herb thought you had a better chance in the longer race," he said. "And you don't want to take a chance getting hurt in the 1500."

"You don't get hurt in the 1500," Twig said, looking away. There was a hint of anger in his voice.

We were in time to watch the 1500, and we settled in the area of the field set aside for athletes. Coach told us to look to see who the press was talking to. "That'll be the favorite," he said.

We watched. Numbers 325 and 301 had all the reporters around them.

"They're both graduates of the University of Portland," Coach said. "They've got a great distance program out there and about five times as many races as they have on the East Coast."

"Where's Portland?" Twig asked.

"Oregon." Coach looked at Twig. "That's north of California, almost near Canada."

"That's a state?"

Coach Day looked at Twig and didn't answer.

"Portland's a city in Oregon," I said.

Number 325 was a dude named LeFebre, and 301 was a skinny black guy who looked African. There were two other Africans in the field of twelve.

At the start of the 1500, the Africans, running together, took the lead. I wondered if they had a plan to work together to win the race. At the end of the first lap, they were still leading and the two guys from Portland were right behind them.

The second lap saw the distance between the first five runners and the rest of the field widen a bit.

"The time is fast," Coach Day said. "I heard LeFebre has a good kick."

On the third lap one of the Africans dropped back and the two guys from Portland moved into third and fourth place. Twig kept checking the scoreboard for the lap times, and he banged my leg with his fist at the beginning of the fourth and final lap.

"It's fast enough to keep the guys from Portland honest," Twig said. "If the black guys can keep it going, it's going to come down to the last two hundred yards."

LeFebre started picking up the pace and caught the African running second on the straightaway. He passed him easily, but then the guy, realizing he had been passed, picked up his pace and was on LeFebre's tail.

It was the first African, who had led most of the way, who faded badly on the turn. He had looked good all the way but fell back to the middle of the trailing pack in a few seconds. The African who LeFebre had passed now gained some ground, and it looked like he might catch him.

"He moved out legal!" Twig said.

"What?"

"LeFebre changed lanes, and the black guy has to move outside or take a chance running late," Coach Day said. "Now there's no place to go inside—he's got to move outside, but he's taking too long."

I watched as LeFebre pumped his arms over the last fifteen yards and won by six feet. The other guy from Portland had moved easily into third place and the two guys embraced just past the finish line.

"What was the move about?" I asked Twig.

"He moved just enough to make the black guy change path," Twig said. "He was clear when he did it, but that messes with your momentum. You have to wait until he makes his move, gets a new path, and that takes a few seconds off the clock."

"He's an experienced runner," Coach Day said.

It was an hour and thirty minutes before the 3000. Coach and I had hamburgers, and Twig had a half container of yogurt. Then Twig stretched as we watched some huge high school shot-putters do their thing in the infield.

When the officials called for the runners of the 3000, I was stupid scared.

"Run your little heart out, man," I said.

"Watch the pace," Coach said. "Keep his ass honest."

"Who?" Twig asked.

"Both of the guys from Portland are in this race and two of the Africans," Coach said. "Expect them to do better, too. Blacks like the longer distances."

"They did the 1500 in 3:58," Twig said. "That ain't walking."

"This won't be walking, either," Coach said.

Twig went over to the starting line, leaned over with his hands on his knees, then stood up and came over to me. He looked distracted, pale.

"I think I'm going to throw up!" he said. "I don't think this race is for me, Darius."

"No, Twig, look at me, friend. Look at me!" I took him by the shoulders and we were face-to-face. "You're never going to reach a point when you don't give a fuck! You will *always* give a fuck, Twig. Just care now, just care today. That's all I'm asking. That's all you got to ask of yourself."

"You in this race, boy?" A thin, bright-eyed official.

"Yeah," Twig said. "I'm in it!"

Twig was starting on one of the outside lanes, but I didn't think it would hurt him because of the distance. Still, I would have liked to see him closer to LeFebre, who was in the third lane. The skinny black guy, who I figured might have been American, was next to Twig. The two Africans were starting from the middle and I wondered if the judges had put them there to give them an advantage.

The race started at a frantic pace, with all of the runners moving inside and getting their positions before the first turn. I looked for Twig and at first couldn't find him. Then I saw him fourth from the rear.

At the end of the first lap all the runners had kept their early positions, with the two Africans again taking the lead. Twig had said that the pace in the 1500 had been hard and I wondered if he should have run that race instead of the tougher 3000.

They started the second lap at 1:01, and the field began to stretch on the turn. My mouth was so dry I had to keep swallowing.

When they crossed the line for the end of the third lap, the runners were stretched over a quarter of the track.

"They're a second over three minutes," Coach Day said. "He can't keep this up."

Twig looked okay. The Africans were still working the lead, taking turns being out front, drafting off each other. LeFebre was third, four yards behind them, and Twig had moved up to fifth.

"If one of the Africans gets tired . . . ," I started to say.

"Don't bet on them getting tired," Coach said. "It's

that fourth guy that we have to worry about."

"You think Twig's got a chance?"

"For fourth?" Coach shrugged his shoulders. "I didn't expect this pace."

Four minutes and two seconds. It was an incredible 1500. I could feel the excitement among the spectators. On the sidelines, pudgy guys with stopwatches were checking them and writing in their notebooks. Herb was right. If Twig could get up for fourth, he had something going on.

At the end of the sixth lap, one African fell back to third, behind LeFebre and the other African. Twig was still fifth.

I tried to think of something, some mental picture I could send him. Coach Day, beside me, was getting excited. He couldn't stay still, leaning against the railing, straightening up, and then leaning again.

"If he doesn't tighten up, he's got a chance," he said.

Twig, don't tighten up! You're as light as a bird. You feel the warm breeze lifting you. You've caught an updraft high above the cinder track. You're lighter than air. You're flying, flying!

The seventh lap ended with LeFebre in the lead.

The other guy from Portland was second and Twig had moved up to third, in front of the African who had been leading. I thought of how LeFebre had cut off the runner in the 1500 and wondered if Twig could get clear.

They rounded the turn with the first three runners putting some distance between themselves and the field. Twig had a chance for third!

On the far straightaway, they were bunched for a moment, and then Twig moved into second place. But he turned his head and looked toward the finish line. Was he done? The second guy from Portland was still on his tail and the other Africans were moving up again.

LeFebre looked strong and I could see him swinging his arms out as he lengthened his stride. Now they were at the top of the track, with less than seventy yards to the finish. Then everybody was pushing forward, edging toward the track as Twig made his move. He was stride for stride with LeFebre; then LeFebre lunged forward for a step, slowed for a step to regain his balance, and went across the finish line a half stride behind Twig!

Twig was on the ground. Guards and judges were

holding the spectators back as the other runners finished.

When Coach and I got to him, he was sitting up. The tears streaming down his face, his shoulders shaking from the sobs.

"Oh, man, I am so happy!" he was saying. "Oh, *man*, I am so friggin' happy!"

"I can't believe it!" I said. "No, I mean I *can* believe it!"

Twig couldn't walk more than five steps without stopping and closing his eyes to get into the moment.

Some reporters were babbling to him, asking him questions about how he felt and whether he'd believed he really had a chance at the start of the race. I could see my friend struggling to find the words he needed, to find ways of getting his feelings into some kind of sense that would satisfy the mikes being pushed his way.

"I thought maybe I had a chance—I always think—there were some really good runners in this race, and, and—" Fists clenched, eyes closed. "I am so happy!"

Coach and I finally got Twig away from the reporters. We went into the locker room, and there were just one or two reporters hanging out and drinking sodas. LeFebre was also there and came over and shook Twig's hand.

"Nice race," he said without moving his lips or looking directly at Twig.

Twig nodded in return.

The rest of the day was crazy. When we got back to the hotel to pick up our bags, Herb, Sean, and Willie were in the lobby talking to some other guys and a tall blond woman. The woman had her clipboard in front of her, scribbling as fast as she could. Herb had Willie standing and was talking about his wrists when we came up.

"He's got the wrist of a fully grown man!" he was saying. "That's all going to translate into pure fucking power one of these days."

"How's his joints?" the woman asked. "I had a kid from Iowa who ran a nine-nine and was out for the season the first time he was hit."

"Tight as a drum!" Herb replied. "Tight as a drum."

Willie was smiling all over himself, but I started thinking they were trying to sell my man, not get him a scholarship.

"He won!" Coach Day said, interrupting Herb's spiel. "Passed LeFebre in the last fifty and took the whole thing!"

Herb looked at Coach Day and then over at Twig. "He *won* the 3000?" he asked, as if he didn't believe it.

"It's going to be on the news this evening," Coach said. "The newspeople were all over him. He ran the best race of his life."

Willie grabbed Twig and started hugging him, and Herb was immediately on the phone. Then he was on two phones and telling one of the other guys who to call.

Twig was a hero.

Sean, the hurdler, had lost his race and was working hard to keep smiling.

Herb kept Willie in Delaware while he made more calls and Coach, me, and Twig got a cab back to the Amtrak station and headed home.

For the whole two hours we were on the train, Coach couldn't shut up, and Twig couldn't talk, but you could see how good he was feeling just by looking at his face. It was wonderful.

I got home and told Mom and Brian as much about the race as I could remember. I told them that Willie had done all right, too. When the phone rang, I almost knew it was going to be Twig.

"Yo, Darius, you know how happy I am and stuff?"

"Yeah, I do," I said. "I really do."

"Darius, I'm happy, but in a way I'm not happy," Twig said. "It's like there's a different me than anybody sees that's happy. You know what I mean?"

"No."

"Me neither, man, but it's almost the same thing so I'm not worried about it," Twig said. "You know what my grandmother said? She said she was going to pray for me, but then she figured I didn't need it. What you think about that?"

"Grandmothers are always cool, Twig," I said.

"Yeah, that's true," Twig said. "You know, you're getting to think like a real Dominican. Maybe next year you'll learn how to dance."

chapter twenty-four

Mom warned me again about being so high on Twig winning. She reminded me that my friend, and not me, had won the race. But in a way, I felt that I had won it, too. Twig had done something from way inside himself and had been successful. But even more, he had shown it could be done.

Mom was strutting the edge. She was right and she knew it, but it wasn't working for me. She had to know that, too. She was dealing with me as if I was a kid and she was the wise old owl. Yo, Mom, I can think for myself! I'm not a kid anymore! What she didn't know was just how far away from being a kid I was. Being a kid wasn't how old you were, it was what you were dealing with in your life. I was dealing with Twig calling me and saying it wasn't him that was so happy, it was another Twig, but it was almost the same. I didn't get my head around it all at once, but it was like right on the edge of my thinking. As if all I needed was some light, or to squint my eyes, and I would see it.

I kept running the race through my head. It always came out the same way, with Twig catching the lead guy at the end and running past, so I let myself go through it over and over. But then I kind of figured it out and I called Twig. He was eating supper and I told him I'd call him later.

"No, I can talk," he said. "What's up?"

"You remember saying how you were happy but not happy at the same time?" I asked.

"I remember."

"The Twig who ran, who worked for that race, that's the happy Twig," I said. "That's your best Twig. The other Twig, the one who has to deal with Midnight and Tall Boy—"

"And my uncle."

"Right, that Twig's a different person," I said. "That's like your history and your neighborhood and shit, and you can't change that part of you. But the part you could change, the getting into condition and finding the heart to take the pain, that's got to be wonderful."

"That could be, Darius," Twig said. "I'm going to have to run it around the track a little bit, but that could be. Now I got to go eat. Shall I eat for two Twigs?"

"Twig, that is so stupid."

"Yeah, I know," he said. I could imagine his smile.

In school some of the freshman girls started a thing, pointing at Twig. It was cool—they would just stop where they were in the hallways when they saw him, hold out their arms, shoulder high, and point at him. Soon all the girls in the school were doing it and some of the guys, too.

Some of the black girls started pointing at Willie, but all of the girls pointed at Twig. He was a little embarrassed at first, but he was liking it at the same time.

"That dude Herb called me," Twig said. We were drifting toward the media center to see a flick on insects that eat other insects. "He said I shouldn't talk to anybody who calls me who says they heard about me winning in Delaware. He says it's illegal."

"But he can call you?"

Twig grinned. "I guess."

"How you like being a star?"

"The star part"—Twig shook his head—"it's not me, but I like it."

I saw Tall Boy and Midnight in the hallway and wondered how they would react. I thought they would screw up, and I was right. Midnight brushed by Twig, pushed him into the wall, and kept walking as if he hadn't noticed him. He had noticed him, all right.

Twig didn't let it get him down, but it messed with me. There were people who didn't want any of us to get away from the crappy little universes they had created for themselves. I wanted to say something to Twig about Midnight and Tall Boy, but I didn't want to stay with it any longer than I had to. Meanwhile, Twig kept saying that his winning the race wasn't all that much, but he couldn't stop talking about it. That made me feel good.

chapter twenty-five

"So he's tapping his head with his finger," Twig said. Him, me, and Brian were walking past the bank toward the valley on 145th. "Like this." He made a squinchy face and touched the side of his head very slowly.

"Your uncle?"

"Yeah, and he's telling me the only reason he didn't want me to run before was that I wasn't thinking," Twig went on. "But now I'm thinking so he's behind me."

"You've got to be kidding me."

"But meanwhile, my grandmother is behind him making the same face and tapping her head the same way he's doing it, and I'm trying not to crack up because she's so funny! And she can imitate anybody! So I'm looking at him and trying to keep a straight face, but it's okay because he don't see anybody except himself anyway."

"I bet one day he's going to want to race you," Brian said.

"He can't run," Twig said. "He smokes so much, he can't even walk up a flight of stairs without wheezing and stopping to catch his breath."

There was a small knot of people in front of the entrance to the park, and I nudged Brian and pointed across the street. "Let's cross," I said.

"Isn't that Midnight?" Brian asked.

I didn't want to look, but I had to. We were less than twenty feet away from where Midnight was standing against the black iron bars. There was an older man standing in front of him. The guy was heavy, with a gut that hung over his belt.

"You said you were going to give her the money for the rent!" Midnight's voice was high, pleading.

"What you in my face for?" The man's voice was husky, slurred. "Why don't you get a damn job?"

"Why did you say you were going to give her the money if you weren't?" Midnight said.

"Go on home, kid," another man said. "Let it go! Let it go!"

"What you want me to tell Mama?"

The punch came fast and hard. It caught Midnight square in the face. I felt Twig's hand on my arm.

"Let's go," he said.

"Johnny, let it go, man." The man who had told Midnight to leave was trying to calm the older man down. "Let it go, man!"

The second blow came, and the third, in quick succession. Midnight tried to twist away, but the man kept punching him in the head and the back of his neck.

"Yo, that's your kid, Johnny," the peacekeeper said. "Let it go before you hurt him."

A police siren sounded, and a black-and-white slowed down. The small crowd that had gathered began to disperse quickly. I watched Midnight slide along the fence and then begin to go down the hill. The man who had been trying to prevent the incident put his arms around Midnight's father and turned him away from his son.

The black-and-white sounded its siren again, waited until the crowd had broken up more, and then began to roll slowly up the hill.

chapter twenty-six

"Today we are going to discuss how Shakespeare created characters to symbolize different aspects of his themes but also reflected his time and culture. In particular, we are going to examine the symbols represented in *The Tempest* by two different characters, Antonio and Caliban. Mr. Elliot, assuming that you have read the assigned text, will you begin our discussion?"

"Yeah, Prospero forgave his brother, Antonio, even though the dude messed him over and really tried to murder him. I think he forgave his brother because he wanted to get back to Europe and get into the good life again," Jimmy said. "He didn't forgive Caliban because he was still mad at him because he was trying to do the nasty with his daughter. So the symbolism is if you're white, you're all right, but if you're black, you *got* to stay back."

"I don't see why you have to bring race into everything," Sara said. "Shakespeare didn't care about race. He was making a point about how people could change. Antonio changed because Prospero gave him his duke position back, but Prospero said Caliban couldn't change. Remember that line about his nurture couldn't affect his nature? Something like that? He couldn't forgive Caliban because Caliban was always going to be who he was."

"What do you think, Darius?" Miss Carroll asked.

"The fact that Shakespeare didn't care about race—if that really is a fact—doesn't mean that he didn't have attitudes about people based on race," I said. "So what's the difference?"

"Well, I don't think Shakespeare was a racist," Miss Carroll said. "But can we get away from name-calling and get to the text we're supposed to be studying?"

"Yo, Teach, if you're going to fight with Darius, can I be the new suck-up?" Jimmy asked.

"Jimmy, that is so pathetic," Miss Carroll said, shaking her head. "Darius has a right to think what he wants. What he needs to do in this class is to organize his thoughts coherently so that they become clear in the context of our studies."

"Hey, Darius, you got that?" Sara asked.

What did I think? I thought about Caliban in the forest of the ghetto, teaching Prospero how to survive, how to hold his child up to the new moon and give her a name.

Call her Miranda, call her love.

What did I think of Prospero looking at Caliban's dark form and thinking him only half human?

"You said you were going to give her the money for the rent!"

Even if the money had been forthcoming, it was too little, too late, to touch the nature of Caliban.

chapter twenty-seven

"They arrested DaSheen!" Heavy-hipped Wanda was sitting on the stoop, yelling into her cell phone. "They caught him with that man's phone and picked him up this morning. Yeah. Yeah. Um-hmm. He's saying he bought it from somebody. They had cops all over the place this morning. They even snatched some guys from the barbershop. You don't be stealing a phone from no white man when they can track it down."

The "white man" was a young Chinese doctor who worked down at Harlem Hospital. He had been confronted by "three hoodies" and stabbed twice in the leg and arm when he tried to resist being robbed. That had been Thursday afternoon. On Friday morning, they arrested DaSheen.

DaSheen Willis was all right. He was nineteen and hung out on the corner most of the time. Sometimes he worked for the Latino furniture store on East 125th Street, delivering furniture, and sometimes he hustled weed, but generally he seemed like a nice guy. I was surprised that he was the one arrested with the phone, and even more shocked when he was released late Friday night.

On Saturday morning, he was shot and killed on his front steps.

The police, in full attack gear, flooded the neighborhood. All the rituals of death started immediately. Mrs. Willis, DaSheen's mother, wailed on the street corner with his aunt, like a two-person Greek chorus. People who hardly knew DaSheen had begun building little memorials to him. Someone had an old picture of him, which was propped against a streetlamp and surrounded with cards and squat colored candles. Signs reading R.I.P. and DASHEEN, WE LOVE YOU were carelessly put against the base of the light so that they looked like a crudely made quilt. A news team showed up, and several of the young people pointed out DaSheen's family, but the camera people weren't interested in the family. They were still pursuing the robbery of the doctor.

"The only story they're going to do is something about how 'gentrification' might not work in Harlem," Sammy said, still wearing his barbershop whites. "When you see it on the news, just remember you heard it here first."

"You don't think he had anything to do with that doctor being stabbed?" I asked.

"It don't hardly matter what he did or didn't do," Sammy answered. "Sometimes it seems to me that all you young folks are taking numbers and getting on line to march yourself down to the graveyard. You're either killing each other or getting killed. It gets discouraging after a while. It does."

"And we're all in the same shadow, and we all smell the same," I said.

"I think I know where you're going with that, Darius," Sammy said. "But just seeing it don't make a difference. We all see it, but we're still marching. Ain't we?"

A truck marked ATHOS FLORIST pulled up, and for a moment, I thought someone had sent flowers for DaSheen's memorial. Then the door opened and I saw it was full of more police in SWAT gear. People started clearing the streets as the cops got out and formed a skirmish line. Two other police cars showed up on the corners and blocked off the street.

"Get off the street, Darius," Sammy said, wiping his hands on his legs. "Just in case these fools get gun-happy."

The police were in front of my house, so I walked as casually as I could across the street into another building. I wanted to see what was going to happen next, but I didn't want to be too close.

It was an old walk-up, a woman from our church lived in it, and I was surprised at how clean it was. The tin was coming off some of the steps, but the halls, although dim, were swept and smelled of cleaning fluid.

The door to the roof was shut, but I saw that a piece of cardboard, folded, had been put at the top of the door to keep it closed. I pushed it open carefully. When I saw there was no one on the roof, I stepped out, put the cardboard back on top of the door, and closed it behind me.

The wind swirled around the roof and I felt goose bumps rise on my arms. Edging my way to the front of the roof, I looked down on the street below.

Fury looks down at the earth from where he flies in slow, lazy circles. He sees each movement below and interprets its meaning. The police are lining up in front of a house they plan to enter. Sharpshooters are crouched behind a police car and the florist van. They must have the name of their prey.

But they could be prey as well.

I watched as the police went cautiously into the apartment building. Then I saw more cops on the roofs across the street from where I watched.

A loudspeaker blared a warning in the street below for people to clear the area. Nobody moved. No cop wanted to confront the crowd of blade-thin dudes as they gathered to watch the action. Younger boys were already make-believe shooting at one another. From where I watched, I could see fingers pointing and kids clutching their stomachs and falling dramatically to the ground, only to get up a moment later to resume their game.

Then I saw cops coming out of the building. One, then two, then two more. Behind them, hands cuffed behind his back, was a young black man in a torn T-shirt and baggy pants. I didn't recognize him, and in a way, I felt I wasn't supposed to recognize him. He was just another black dude being busted.

The police put him over the hood of their patrol car and searched him carefully. The girls started talking, their voices, indistinct from the street below, sounding like the random chatter of birds.

The SWAT team, its members swaggering about in small circles, waited until the patrol cars had left before getting back into the florist van. Soon they, too, were gone, and the traffic across 145th Street resumed.

I had started to go downstairs when I thought about what I had seen from my roof, looking across the street. I glanced over to where I would have been sitting if I'd been on my own building. I saw the chimney a few feet away. From where I stood, it looked like all the other roof structures. I walked to it.

There was gray packing tape on one brick. I looked around to see if there were other eyes watching me. I pulled the packing tape, and the brick came away. I reached into the small opening and touched the gun.

Evil has a feel, a coldness. I felt sick. I walked stiffly down the stairs.

Home.

* * *

Twig called.

"I heard something went down on your block," he said.

"Police stuff," I said. "Fifty cops running around trying to look tough and waving all kinds of automatic weapons. It looked like Vietnam or something. They arrested somebody."

"You don't know who?"

"Male, white T-shirt, dark skin, either African American or Latino, didn't finish high school but plans on taking his GED in the fall if he's not in jail," I said.

"Twenty-five years to life!" Twig said.

"What's going on with you?" I asked, sensing he was down.

"Nothing much," Twig said. "I don't know— I hoped I'd feel different after I won in Delaware. Things slipped back to normal so quick."

"The girls stopped pointing at you?"

"Some still do and it makes me smile, man," Twig said. "I like that, but it doesn't mean anything. I'm still the same Twig. The race is already history. But I'm still running it at night. In my head, I'm still tracking down that dude and wondering if I'm going to pass him."

"He's thinking about it too," I said. "I bet he's got a picture of your face in his mind."

"You think?"

"Yeah," I said. "Hey, you remember Mr. Watson saying that he thought some guys hid guns on the roof?"

"Yeah?"

"I know where they hide them," I said.

"It won't do you any good," Twig said. "You're not a gun man. You're like that bird of yours, what's his name?"

"Fury."

"Yeah, Fury, flying so high above the streets you can't even make out the people below."

"That's your vision? Can you imagine a falcon flying that high?" I asked.

"Yeah."

"Me too," I said. "That Herb guy call you again?"

"He calls me every day," Twig said. "Says he just wants to check up on me. How's my family and stuff. I'm, like—*spooked*!"

"You scared of him?"

"No, I don't think so," Twig said. "But I don't know what his game is. And maybe I don't know enough about what big-time racing is all about. I don't want to do anything stupid if I think I got a chance to do something good. That make sense?"

"Yeah, it does."

"I thought it would make sense to you," Twig said.

We say good-bye and hang up and I take out my story from the Salvation Army bookcase my father bought for me before he walked.

At last I am feeling what the boy felt in the water. The tide is pushing him away from the shore and the dolphins might or might not be waiting for him just beyond the edge of his endurance. But there is not one boy, there are at least two in that body struggling against the cold tide. One has faith in himself, the other faith in what he might be. If things were different. If there were other chances. If his father hadn't walked. If the rent had been paid. If this. If that.

What had Twig said? He was happy but it was not him who was happy? The Twig who was happy was the one I had known for so many years. The one who wanted to run and to feel good about himself. That was the happy Twig. The other one, the one who Coach talked about, the one who told himself that just finishing fourth in Delaware would be enough because it was what they wanted him to do, that was a different Twig.

I looked at the story again, imagining the boy swimming away from the shore, wanting to turn back to see how far he had gone, afraid to turn back, afraid to stop and afraid not to stop his journey beyond his own abilities. I knew the difference. Now I just had to write it.

chapter
twenty-eight

There is a relationship between the raptor and its prey. Both have a combination of instinct and survival skills and both are, in the end, resigned to their respective fates, their individual experiences. It is only when one, or both, are human, that learning happens and the balance is changed.

"What's up, man?" Ten thirty p.m., and from the ringtone I know it's Twig. "I thought athletes were supposed to get eight hours of sleep."

"You hear what happened over at Rucker Park?"

"No, I've been home all evening," I said. I looked over to where Brian was sleeping and saw that he had his notebook in bed with him.

"Midnight and some jerks from his posse were over there, and then some guys from the projects hit the park and started shooting," Twig said. "You know Joleen Harris?"

"Dark girl with pretty eyes?" I asked. "You were hanging with her?"

"No, she called Vanessa, my cousin, and said that Midnight got shot in the stomach," Twig said. "My cousin called me and told me."

"Is he dead?"

"No, he ran out of the park, but they say he was bleeding bad," Twig said. "Nobody knows where he is now. Some of his homeys went to his house and he wasn't there, and they called around to hospitals and stuff like that."

"This just happened?"

"About two hours ago, but my cousin just called me."

"He's probably not hurt too bad if he ran from the park," I said.

"I don't know. My cousin Vanessa said that Joleen, who was on the scene, said he was bleeding from his stomach," Twig said. "There was blood on his T-shirt, and she thought he was bleeding from the mouth, too."

"Damn!"

"That's just what I was thinking," Twig said. "They said the fools who lit him up were Young Disciples. They were out to send somebody to the table!"

"I hear that," I said. The table down at the morgue was the last place a lot of dudes from the nabe reached. "I thought they were trying to clean Rucker up. You think Midnight's really wasted?"

"I don't know. You would think he would either head home or to a hospital, right?" Twig said.

"Was Tall Boy in the park?" I thought about seeing Midnight get slapped around by his father and thought that maybe home wasn't the best place for him to go.

"I don't know, but that's where the cops went looking for him," Twig said. "And they still didn't find him. Maybe he's thinking that if they wanted to kill him, they're still looking for him."

"And don't know how bad they got him already," I said.

"Something like that."

"He'd go to a safe place. You don't shoot somebody and then run to their turf to look for them," I said. "Did the whole thing take place in the park?"

"Not according to what Joleen told my cousin,"

Twig said. "But I don't really know, because my cousin was all excited telling me about it."

"She knows you and Midnight don't cut it?"

"No, but Vanessa's only fourteen so she got all excited and happy to run her mouth," Twig said. "Then I got Joleen's number and called her and she was mad at Vanessa because she called everybody and told them before she could."

"I guess we'll hear about it in the morning," I said.

"Yo, Darius, do you think maybe Midnight collapsed somewhere?" Twig asked. "Maybe he panicked when he got shot and ran because he just didn't want to lay down and get shot some more."

"The Young Disciples stayed in the park?"

"No, Joleen said everybody was running and climbing fences and stuff," Twig said. "I think if I had been there, I'd've jumped over the fence! When shots are going off, you can't sit around and check out everything. The police are out on the street now, so there won't be any more banging tonight."

"You thinking Midnight just went somewhere and collapsed?"

"Could be," Twig said. "I don't know. What else could he do? I don't think he's got a girlfriend."

Brian stirred and sat up.

"What's going on?" he asked. "Is Mama home?"

"It's Twig on the phone," I said. "Yeah, everything's okay. Mama is home. Midnight got shot and they don't know where he is."

"Brian up?" Twig asked.

"Yeah. Look, maybe Midnight went someplace to hide," I said. "I've seen Diablo and some of them on the roof across from me."

"Across from you? Midnight don't live there."

"No, but I've seen them on one of the roofs," I said. "Down from the supermarket."

"I don't think so," Twig said. "If you were hurting bad, you wouldn't run up on a roof. If somebody caught him up there, they could just throw him off."

"Not if he had a gun," I said.

"Joleen said he didn't have a gun," Twig went on. "She said when the Young Disciples—and yo, Darius, I don't know if it was really the Young Disciples, because when I asked Joleen, she didn't know the guy who was doing the shooting—but Midnight wasn't shooting back or anything so I don't think he had a gun."

"There's a gun up on the roof," I said.

"You don't know that," Twig said.

"Yeah, I do," I said. "Midnight might have gone

up on the roof to get a gun and then couldn't make it down again. I'm going up on my roof and see if he's there."

"You serious?"

"I'll call you back," I said.

"Yo, Darius, why you getting into this? This is some crazy shit, but you don't want to get involved in this, right?" Twig asked.

"I don't know, Twig," I said. "Maybe I do."

Twig asked me if I was serious again, and I told him I was. Then I hung up and started putting my pants on.

"Where you going?" Brian asked.

"Up on the roof."

"Now?"

"Yeah, now shut up."

"I'm telling Mama."

"She was drinking again," I said. "You won't be able to wake her. And if you do, you'll just get her more upset. You want to do that?"

"I don't want you to go out now." Brian's voice sounded even younger than it usually does.

"I just need to check on something," I said. "I'll be right back. You make sure the door is locked behind me. And sit near the door to open it fast if I tell you to, okay?"

"Why you got to go out, Darius?"

I laced my sneakers as fast as I could, grabbed my phone, and headed for the door. I waited a second until I heard Brian click the lock, and then I started up the two flights to the roof.

The stairs up the first flight, to the fifth floor, were the same as the steps all the way down to the lobby. The steps from the fifth floor to the roof looked older, and the linoleum was cracked and broken in spots. The door to the roof was bolted shut, and I felt good about that.

I slipped the bolt back and eased the door open. It was dark. The odors of old tar, rain, and rotting garbage rising from the alley between the buildings mixed, making me feel slightly nauseous. Easing over to the edge of the roof, I felt myself straining to be taller, so that I could see over the low wall even before I got to it.

I could feel myself breathing hard as I touched the rough concrete barrier that separated the roof of my building from the one next to it. Two buildings down, a clothesline with some light-colored clothes on it flapped in the wind, startling me. I imagined them to be shirts. The roof across the street was not quite as dark as mine. Looking where I had found the gun, I concentrated on the shadows. I didn't see anything at first and felt relieved. Then I saw what looked, from where I sat shivering, like a sheet of plywood or an old door lying at an angle against a wall. There was something sticking out from under the door. The rain was picking up and it was hard to see. It could have been a brick. Or a bottle. Or the bottom of a shoe.

Twig on speed dial!

"How you know it's Midnight?" he said. "It could be a homeless guy or a crackhead."

"Or it could be just an old shoe," I said. "But I'm going over there to find out."

"Why?" Up-front. To the point. Why?

"Twig, it's something about . . . something about the best me that I can be—"

"You're going to get yourself in a mess, Darius," Twig said. "You got to ask yourself if Midnight—if that's Midnight—is worth it."

"No, I got to ask myself what I'm about," I said.

"You sure about this?"

"No, Twig, but I gotta do it," I said. "You don't have to come with me."

Downstairs. I didn't want to stop to tell Brian what I was doing. If it was nothing, a shoe, a homeless guy, a crackhead, then I'd come back and let him know what had happened.

chapter twenty-nine

In the street, the rain was picking up. The street was less crowded than earlier. There were people going into the bodega on the corner, some standing on the corner, their bodies at odd angles under their three-dollar umbrellas, waiting for their connections to show up with whatever got them through the night. I walked to the corner and crossed, trying to look as if I weren't scared.

Down the street I saw Twig coming toward me. He had on his hoodie from school, and I waited until he reached the corner.

"Yo, Darius, I'm thinking this is serious stupid," Twig said.

"Maybe." I was glad as anything to see him.

The hallway at 176 was bright. The freshly painted yellow walls were almost cheerful as Twig and I went upstairs. On the third floor, a door was open and I could hear a baby crying.

The top floor, the cardboard stuck between the door and the jamb to keep it closed, the cool night air.

"We got a plan?" Twig whispered.

"We call out his name," I whispered back. "So we don't surprise him."

"Suppose there's somebody else here with him?"

Shit! I was losing my nerve again. I walked slowly toward where I had seen what I had imagined was plywood from my roof. Up close, I could see it was cardboard. I saw the foot and pointed toward it to show Twig.

"Hey, Midnight!"

There was a noise that sounded like a grunt, or maybe even a fart. Then the cardboard moved and I saw Midnight struggling to rise up to one elbow. He was pushing up with his left hand, the one without the gun.

"You okay, man?"

"Back up, bitch!" He was wheezing, inhaling sharply between each word. "I'll blow your ass off!"

"You need some help!" Twig said.

"What you guys doing? You coming up here to have sex?"

"Come up here looking for you," I said. "How you doing?"

"I don't need . . ." Midnight looked around, trying to get his bearings. "You got Tall Boy's number?"

"You don't need Tall Boy," I said. "You need a doctor. You going to die up here. Everybody was looking for you. They were calling your house and calling Tall Boy's crib."

"What he say?"

"He said the same thing everybody else was running down, that you and him got into it with some dudes and the shots went off. Then he split," I said. "Twig and I figured you might have come up here and maybe needed some help."

"Fuck you!"

"Whatever, I'm going to call 911!"

"No you ain't!" Midnight lifted the gun and pointed it at me. "Call Tall Boy!"

"What's he going to do if he does come up here?" I asked. "He's not a doctor. You look like you're about ready to check out."

Midnight's head went down and the gun was pointed down at the tarred roof. He was breathing hard and trying to sit up.

"Why don't you just lay still and let us get some help?" Twig asked.

"Why?"

"So you can be alive tomorrow," I said.

Midnight made a noise, almost a crying noise, like a wounded animal. He was a rabbit caught somewhere in the wilds, and a raptor had him. He was helpless and he knew it.

He looked around wildly. His face was twisted, and the blood on his lower lip made him look weird in the dim light.

"You got to get rid of the gun," Midnight said. "We can't get caught with no gun."

"I'll get rid of it," Twig said. He took the gun from Midnight.

I dialed 911 and told the operator where I was and that a teenager had been shot and needed help bad. She wanted to know who all was on the roof, and I gave her our three names. Then she asked me if there were any guns on the roof, and I said no.

I watched as Twig took the gun, holding it with a

ballpoint pen through the trigger guard, and took it to another roof, stepping over the low barriers that separated the buildings. He didn't make any effort to hide it, and I knew we could always call in an anonymous tip later. I thought it would be okay if the police found it there.

The rain picked up and Twig took off his hoodie and wrapped it around Midnight's shoulders.

"How you know about this place?" Midnight asked me.

"Everybody knows about this place," I lied. I wasn't afraid anymore, but I didn't want Midnight to think I was the only one who had seen where they hid guns.

"Young Disciples shot my ass," Midnight said. "They were looking for somebody named Duke. My name ain't no damned *Duke*. A bunch of stupid assholes shot me and I wasn't even who they were looking for! That's some foul shit!"

"Yeah." Twig.

"How come you guys come up here?" Midnight caught his breath and grimaced. He was hurting bad. "What time is it, anyway?"

I waited until his breath had got back to normal before looking at my watch. "Yo, Midnight, don't worry—it's not midnight yet!"

"That ain't funny, faggot!"

Midnight, on the roof. I could see his hand begin to shake a little and I wondered if he was going to make it. On TV cop shows, they always showed the victim being taken to the hospital and added "where he died" or something.

We heard the sirens first. Then my cell rang and it was the police. We told them we were still on the roof. They asked again about weapons and we said we didn't have any.

The cops came up on the roof first. Two of them, one black and one Latino, pointed their guns at us.

"Move that cardboard!" The Latino cop had his flashlight trained on Midnight.

We had adjusted the cardboard so that it just about covered all of Midnight. When we moved it, we saw his shirt covered with blood. The cops told me and Twig to stand up, and they patted us down as two more cops came up on the roof. Then the EMT guys came on the roof, put on blue rubber gloves, and started working on Midnight.

"You guys shoot him?" the black cop asked me.

We told him we hadn't, that we all went to the

same school and we had heard he had been shot.

"Nobody knew where he was," I said. "I thought he might be up here."

"You smoke crack up here?"

"No, I don't smoke crack anywhere!" I said.

They gave Midnight some kind of shot and put him on a stretcher. Two cops went down first, then the emergency guys carrying Midnight, then the other two cops, with me and Twig following.

When we got to the street, there was a small crowd and the Latino cop asked some people some questions, pointing to me and Twig. They had already taken our IDs and addresses and said they would pick us up if necessary.

"Anything you got to say, you'd better say it now!" The black cop got into my face.

"I don't have anything more to say," I said.

He mean mugged me and then got into a squad car and left.

"My mom is going to go crazy with me out this late," Twig said. We were finally away from the crowd and walking toward Twig's house. "This is one of those nights you can't explain away to your family."

"I think I got it though," I said.

"You're shaking, man—you okay?"

"Just cold," I said.

"What you got?" Twig said. "You said you got something."

"When we were up there on the roof, I was trying to figure out what was going on in Midnight's mind. I imagined him doing what we do when things get bad, trying to reach inside and pull something up. You know what I mean?"

"Whatever you got special," Twig said.

"Yeah. And what I figured out was that when Midnight looked inside, he didn't find anything to pull up."

"So?"

"So when he goes around saying he don't give a fuck, it's because the sucker doesn't have a fuck to give!"

"Did I know that?" Twig asked.

"You might have known the tune, but now you got the words to it, too."

Chapter Thirty

The falcon glides easily over the city. Enjoying the sun on his back, the warm breezes rippling through his feathers. For a moment he is caught in an updraft and allows himself to float aimlessly higher. Turning slightly, he sees a small puff of white cloud above. As he turns even more, the dark shadows of the street are a mosaic, alive, hundreds of feet below. The falcon has already had his meal for the day. Now it is time to just enjoy the flight.

Twig and I spent the week explaining to everybody and their grandmother about finding Midnight on the roof. Mrs. Nixon was particularly upset when the *Amsterdam News* reported that the victim and his rescuers all went to Phoenix. I think she expected the entire police department to come down on the school in force. Nobody came. It wasn't that big a deal to them, just another kid shot in the hood.

Word had gotten around that Twig and I found him, probably through the Twittercy Express. It was also on Joleen's Facebook page.

When Miss Carroll heard about it, she cornered me in the hallway and said I should write about the experience.

"People want to know about the kinds of lives they don't have the chance to see close up," she said.

"I'll think about it," I said.

"Don't be put off because it's black," she said.

Thursday afternoon and me and Twig were at Baker Field. A few real runners were using the track, but most of the kids were just jogging or fooling around. One girl was running with a baby on her back.

"So why did she say that?" Twig asked after I told him what Miss Carroll had said. "She's thinking you don't want to be black?"

"She thinks I don't want to write about black stuff," I said. "But the truth is that I don't want to

192

write about the stuff that *she* thinks is black. White people are always telling you what your life is about and then saying you should write about it."

"You told her that?"

"No, I didn't want to get into a big thing about what was black and what wasn't," I said.

"Maybe you should," Twig said. "A lot of stuff that goes down with us is because you're black and I'm Dominican. People just looking over the fence don't see that."

"You would have jumped all over her?" I asked.

"No, not if I was me." Twig flashed that big smile again. "But if I was you, I would have been on her like *amarillo en arroz*!"

"Twig, that is so stupid."

"Yeah, I know!"

"Read the story," I said.

I had brought my story to Baker Field to show Twig. The revisions had gone well and I thought it worked, but I wanted to know what my friend thought of it. He had already read it three times, so I knew he would see all the changes.

We were sitting on the wooden bleacher seats, and Twig picked up "The Song of a Thousand Dolphins" again. The thing was that I hadn't changed it the way the editor had suggested. What I had done was to make the boy stronger, in a way, but not stronger by relying on the dolphins to make it back to shore. He was reinventing himself, finding the "better" person within. I didn't think the editor was going to go for that too tough, but I wanted Twig to understand it. I wanted even more for him to like it.

"You read slowly," I said, noticing that he was only on the second page.

"Run a mile," he answered.

"What's that mean?"

"I read slow, you run slow," Twig said. "You go out there and run a mile, and by the time you finish, I'll be done reading the story."

He went back to the reading.

The girl carrying the baby passed again. I was sure she was thinking that everyone was looking at her. Some people are like that. They do anything just to get you to look at them.

Out of the corner of my eye, I saw Twig finally move a page to the back of the manuscript.

"You translating it into Spanish?" I asked.

"Run a mile!"

"I can run a mile," I said.

"No you can't," Twig said. "That's four times around. Go!"

I got up and walked onto the track. I could just feel Twig watching me as I did some toe touches. I did seven, and then I started off.

The thing was I didn't know how fast to go. I had run races against other kids, usually in gym, or sometimes against Brian in the park, but not on a track. It couldn't be that hard. Anyway, as slowly as Twig read, I didn't have to put myself out. It was a good day to run. The air coming off the river felt clean and good in my face. Around the first turn I got myself to relax and brought my arms down the way I saw so many runners do. The way Twig ran.

When Twig was at his best, when he was in a race and depending on his own inner strengths, his ability to take the pain and fatigue and to dig inside and pull up the determination to finish strong, he wasn't the same Twig who sat in front of Midnight not daring to turn around. He wasn't the same Twig his uncle could put down, either. The Twig he became when he ran was too much to fit into the neat frame of somebody else's life.

I was making the first turn, and I looked over to where the finish line was.

"If they look over to see where the race finishes, it means they're tired!" Twig had said.

I really wasn't that tired. A little tired. Maybe I would start jogging more.

It didn't matter if the editor didn't like my changes. No, it mattered in a way. If he didn't like my story, if he didn't publish it, then my chances of getting a scholarship went way down. But I couldn't let what he thought define my life. It would be as if a chalk mark around a body were all there was to define the life within. The editor had his taste, and his background and his smarts, and that was all good. But I couldn't give up my abilities because they didn't match his taste. No, that wasn't right. Of all the people I was— the guy who didn't want to confront Midnight, the one who felt helpless when his mother drank too much, or the one who panicked when he saw his father on the streets, tightroping his way down some nightmare in his head—I had to pick the best me there was.

I didn't want to speed up when I passed Twig, but I did. A little.

I was tired. The second lap was a lot worse than

the first one. Little waves of nausea came over me. Checking my watch, I saw it was twenty minutes to seven. I didn't know when I had started, but I thought I was probably doing about a 1:10 quarter. Already part of the way through the second lap, it was too late to time the whole quarter, but I thought I'd check it when I passed the start line again.

When me and Twig went up on the roof to find Midnight, I thought that was a best me, and a best Twig. Maybe it wasn't. That was an okay me, yes, but I thought that the best me was somewhere in my words, in my thinking.

Dear God, don't let me throw up.

I crossed the start line. It was eighteen minutes to seven. I was doing more than two minutes a friggin' lap. I ran a little past Twig and sat down on the infield grass. The world was spinning around me, and soon I was telling myself how much I was going to exercise in the future.

I lay there for another ten minutes before Twig came over.

"Yo, Darius, you dead?"

"Yeah."

He sat next to me. I felt something pressing down on my back and realized it was Twig's head. Then he moved and told me my heart wasn't beating that fast.

"You're just out of shape, dude."

"Oh, I hadn't noticed that," I said. "I just thought somebody ran off with all the oxygen."

"I like your story better now," Twig said. "Before, it was good, but there were parts I didn't get. Like why the kid was swimming with a bad leg. And I liked the dolphins—they're like a metaphor, right?"

"Yeah, sort of," I answered. "Only I don't think in terms of metaphors."

"Yeah, you do," Twig said. "You got dolphins and falcons and stuff in all your stories. You can't fly and you—can you swim?"

"No."

"See?"

"Could be."

"But now the story is clearer because the kid is looking for something inside of himself, and that's what it's all about. And you know what else I like about the story? I like the fact that at the end, he still has a bad leg and stuff isn't just wonderful. He's still got all the problems in his life and he's still got to deal with them. Shit doesn't go away easy."

"Like we still have to deal with the stuff in our lives?" I asked.

"That's right," Twig said. "I break my leg or lose a couple of races and where am I? Maybe stacking boxes in a bodega."

"No, I don't think so," I said as I rolled over and sat up. "If you get over once, I mean if you really get over the way you did in Delaware, and the way you did against Jameson, you have to know that there's a best Twig somewhere in you, and you just got to find a chance for him to do his thing. It doesn't have to always be about running."

"Maybe it's about having somebody like your non-running, nonflying, and nondancing butt around to keep reminding me about a best Twig."

"Could be," I said, standing.

"So when are you going to send your story off?" Twig asked.

"I already did," I said. "This morning."

"Before I read it?"

"I was afraid you weren't going to like it," I said.

"If I'm going to be your agent, you always— I repeat, *always*—have to send me the story first," Twig said. "You got that?"

"Yes, sir."

"All right!"

epilogue

In the end, things worked out well for me and Twig. He got two scholarship offers, one from the University of North Carolina and one from Texas Christian. He took the one from Texas Christian because it was a full ride without a loan.

The *Delta Review* took my story and published it. I was excited when I got the acceptance letter but disappointed with the magazine. The copy I had seen of the Canadian publication was printed on slick paper and had nice illustrations. The two copies they sent me were smaller and on cheap paper. Mr. Ramey wasn't impressed and said there wasn't much he could do with it. Miss Carroll was happy with it, though, and sent out both of my copies to friends. The one that she sent to a friend at the English department at Amherst College in Massachusetts resulted in a scholarship offer. It involved a job at the school, some student loans, and a reduced tuition plan.

Midnight only partially recovered from being shot up. He's in a wheelchair, but he did get to move to handicapped housing with his mom and little sister.

I'm going to spend the rest of the year working with Brian. His grades are good and I hope he can keep them up. He's not going to get any help from Mom, I know, but what I'm hoping is that he doesn't get discouraged. As Twig said, the shit in your life doesn't go away easy.

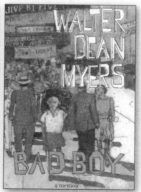